GOLDEN EYED LEGEND

LEGENDARY STARS SAGA BOOK ONE

DAI'JA S. ROSE

NOVA INK BOOKS

GOLDEN EYED LEGEND

LEGENDARY STARS SAGA BOOK ONE

DAI'JA S. ROSE

NOVA INK BOOKS

Contact info: www.daijasrosebooks.com

ISBN (digital): 979-8-9891572-0-4

ISBN (paperback): 979-8-9891572-1-1

Edited by Susan Michaud

Map designed by: Luis Leopardi – Fiverr (leidolfr)

Nova Ink Books

To Mom and Dad, thank you for everything... always.

Kashmala
Wyndhm
Snow Tribe
Beach Tribe
Jungle Tribe
Upper Ember
Lower Ember
THEYRA
PYROC
Mystic Ocean
Kindle

BOOKTOK PRAISE

"This book was a breath of fresh air for fantasy readers. I'm excited to read more of the Legends story!" – @mblazer21

"Prepare to be captivated by this debut fantasy novel brimming with enchanting magic and extraordinary characters. Eagerly awaiting the sequel." – @bookswithambs

"Jai's character had me hooked from the very beginning! Navigating his impossible fate and accepting the reality of his new found purpose was an exhilarating journey. This is one for those who struggle to find intention and those ever faced with a life or death choice. " – @bookbehavior

"The Golden Eyed Legend is a riveting new fantasy series that I simply could not put down!" – @laurenslibraryyy

"Fun, adventurous, and fiery. It was a fast-paced, action pack. Our story is set in a world where some have lost their magic and others have kept and nurtured it. The story centers on a young man named Jai who was orphaned and taken in at a young age. One day he finds out he was gifted with a great power and must begin his adventure to control and protect his new found family and friends. I will say it is a nice debut. It is fast paced and to the point. Which I am always a fan of. It is also heavily ATLA inspired and I am loving the opportunity to jump into a similar world with fun and powerful characters all trying to move forward and discover themselves and their goals." – @theladyravens

"Golden Eyed Legend is the perfect book for a fantasy lover, and the perfect book if you don't know fantasy or are new to it. I love the world building and the characters arcs. Calida was my favorite! I love a strong willed woman! This book gave me Avatar the Last Airbender vibes in the best way! It was action packed and hard to put down as you wanted to continually know what happened next. For a debut novel, especially in fantasy, I can say this checks all the boxes, amazing world building, likeable characters,

great buildup and character arcs and an ability to keep you engaged from the very first chapter. If I had to use one word to describe this book it would be impactful, you feel something from every character and it adds to the story."
– @paristhebibliophile

"I really enjoyed reading this. It's not the typical genre I would normally read, but after reading this it's something I'm interested in reading more! I thought the description, the imagery, and the flow of the book was spectacular. It's very well written for a first time writer! I can't wait to read more from you in the future." – @cheyennetatikaaa

"The world building in the Golden Eyed Legend is intricate and intriguing. I found the magic system unique and an immediate draw. Instantly, I was curious about Jai's backstory and wanted to know more. If you're looking for the next epic fantasy read, this is it!" – @dmcancel
** @dmcancel is the author of *Blood & Sunlight* and *Shadows & Secrets*

Fire is life.

Your purpose is likened to a flame and it fuels your passion.

You are brave and ambitious.

Proactive, never reactive; you rise with the sun.

There is boldness in your blood.

You have no need for fear: your own flames shall never burn you.

Never underestimate the fire of another.

Your heart is made of fire, such that when you marry your purpose, you will always be victorious.

FIREHEARTS

FIRE | LIGHT | HEART

G lorified Universe,

Oh, how I have strayed away. How I forget to pray to the glorious heavens. Forgive me for neglecting you. Shed your light upon me one more time; I will be better. Give my successor a light greater than mine. Make his light undeniable. Let his soul reflect the essence of the Sun: light, warmth, love, and life. Most importantly, life—for without the Sun, there would be no life. Let him embrace this power and cherish it. Do not allow him to follow in my wake of death, continuous mistakes, and failure. Let him learn to harness the power of life and never turn his back on you.

Forgive me, Universe, for having my successor inherit the consequences of my mistakes. I am leaving him a world of turmoil; however, this was not my intention. I only wanted to make a legacy, but now he will experience the consequences of my ambitions. I pray the Fire of the Universe guides him and he never turns his back on the order of the Universe. It took me a long time to recognize and acknowledge my mistakes, and for that, I am truly sorry. I am turning my face to the setting sun and asking for forgiveness. It will be a long night—a dark night. I feel it in the essence of everything that I am. But no night lasts forever. The dawn will come again to usher in a new era of peace.

Universe, when he rises, guide him and light his path as you lit mine. Universe, control the raging wildfires. Restrain the fires of anger, fear, hatred, and pain; make them bow to the light and the fire of life. Will he be like fire? Will he burn? Will he be like fire? Will he bring life? Glorious Universe, only you know. Set upon me peacefully, as I have lived long and learned much. Rise upon him gently; show him his worth. Thank you for blessing me and guiding me through everything. Now my sun is setting into the distant horizon, never to rise again.

   -Cyra

CHAPTER I

*I*n the midday heat, the sun bore down upon the world with an unrelenting intensity. Its rays blazed like a fiery inferno, casting an unforgiving glare that seared my eyes. The sky was painfully bright as if the sun had bleached all color from the world.

The heat was palpable, a thick, heavy weight that pressed down upon everything and everyone. It seemed to suffocate the air, leaving it hot and dry and difficult to breathe. The sun beat down upon the parched earth, causing the ground to crack and split in protest.

With a sea of sand dunes in the distance, my father stood before me, his back facing me. His black pants were barely visible underneath the long, satin burgundy tunic with bold gold trim on its sleeves. On the rocky cliffs where we stood, I darted directly behind his shadow. Finally, there was relief from the beaming sun.

He chuckled as I clung to the back of his robe.

A gentle yet massive hand tousled my black hair, "Jai, remember what I told you. Go to the end of the tunnel and wait for me. I'll come and get you once this business is over."

"Can I just go home?" I didn't want to go. Instead, I gripped the smooth fabric tighter in my small hands, wrinkling the robe.

"No, son, this won't take too long." my father chuckled. "As soon as I'm finished, we are going on our first hunt together, just like I promised. Then we can show your mother the fruits of your labor."

"And I'll get my own bow afterward?"

He turned to me and smiled, those light brown eyes almost glowing in the sunlight. His black curly hair framed his warm brown face, and he laughed, "Of course you will! A hunter needs his own bow. Go along, Jai. I'll come and get you once I'm finished."

"Then you will show me the fire, right? You said it's time I start learning the fire! Will I be great like you?"

"After I handle business," he spoke slowly. He gently pushed me in the direction of the tunnels.

I turned and ran to him, hugging him tight, "Okay, Father, I'll see you soon." I turned to leave before stopping in my tracks, "Father, I hope your business goes well."

"Thank you, son. I'm sure it will."

Suddenly the face of my father became distorted. Twisting until nothing but brown dots danced in my vision. Then there was water—a river? Son? I can only imagine what it means to be a son. That word is so empty. I'm unfit to be called a son. What kind of son forgets his father and mother? If only he would turn to face me one more time. Maybe if I looked into his eyes once more, I'd remember everything I was to him. Everything he was to me. How could I ever forget him?

*****

A sharp pain shot through Jai's head, tearing him from sleep. As he blinked the sleep from his eyes, he realized he had been dreaming—a vivid, surreal dream that left him feeling shaken and disoriented. He looked up and around. The gently shimmering light from the daybreak peeked through the flimsy fabric of his dark red curtains. Besides those small glints of light, his room was completely dark. Jai tossed the bed cover off his body, turning so his feet could touch the floor. Slowly, the remnant of the dream began to slip away, like sand through his fingers. But the feeling it left behind remained—a sense of unease, a feeling of loss. As he tried to recall the dream, he felt a pang of sadness wash over him. As usual, there was something he couldn't quite remember. Instinct told him it was something important. And then it hit him—he couldn't remember his family.

Rubbing his eyes with his warm brown hands truly awakened him to the new day. Jai took a deep breath and forced himself to get out of bed, to face the day ahead. He knew that he had to keep searching for the missing pieces of himself. How could his memories be so deeply locked away? Sadness lingered like a heavy weight on his shoulders; in the depth of his mind, he felt alone.

Finally standing up, he looked around his tiny room complete with a small bed, a worn chest, and a wall mirror. Other than that, he possessed nothing outside of a temperamental gift from the Universe. This gift was more like a nuisance with a mind of its own. He looked down at his hands as if something was supposed to happen, but besides the lines on his palms, there was nothing to see. It felt pointless to be gifted at all. This was his secret. No one could learn of his ability. No one. He would be exiled if anyone ever caught a glimpse of his unruly powers.

Jai's heart was consumed by two things: confusion and guilt—one emotion fueling the other. Eager to free his mind from his misfortunes, Jai opened his wooden door and stumbled through a narrow hallway into the tiny house kitchen. The kitchen was barely larger than his own room. A tall man with black, wavy hair stood with his back facing Jai. Soot and ash covered his clothes. The once maroon-colored pants looked as if they were bought black. Looking down at his own pants, he closed his eyes. His own clothes weren't much better. Stumbling along half-awake, Jai took a seat on the backless wooden stool. Plopping his body down, he tossed his head back and groaned, feeling like the weight of the world was on his shoulders.

"Morning, son," the man spoke without turning around, tending to the small wood stove in the cozy kitchen. The smell of food was making its imprint throughout the house.

"Good morning," Jai sighed and propped his head on the round table with a red linen tablecloth. Being called a son didn't sit right with him. His stomach felt uneasy whenever anyone called him that. However, he longed for that title to eventually have a deeper meaning.

"Don't tell me you had that same dream you can never remember."

Jai chuckled, "Then I guess I have nothing to say."

The man slid a white ceramic plate filled with soft yellow scrambled eggs in front of him along with a tall glass of water. He smiled with contentment dancing in his brown eyes as his tawny brown hand let go of the plate. "Eat up now. We have a big day."

Every day is a big day; there isn't a day when we aren't busy.

"Thank you, Arka. So, what constitutes a big day to you? We stay busy."

"We just got ourselves a large contract, son. An order for five hundred fire daggers and two thousand bombs. That is our largest order to date."

Who could possibly need all of those daggers and bombs? Well, at least we won't have to worry about work as the seasons change. We'll be eating pretty well this winter.

"Okay, now we're talking. With an order like that, winter will be easy. By spring we can finally make that move you've been talking about for years. Are we the only ones working this job, or will a temp worker be helping us out like last time?"

"I'm discussing the project with three young workers today. I can't work my only son to death, can I?" Arka chuckled and gently punched Jai's arm.

"But you'd try," Jai playfully mumbled as he took another bite of his eggs. As they were eating, there was a violent knock on the door. "I'll get it. You eat your breakfast." Jai walked to the door and casually opened it.

A young man with hostile energy peered into the house. He stepped into the house. If Jai hadn't moved, he would have been knocked over. "Arka, I have some business concerning you," he looked at Jai from the corner of his eye, ignored his presence, and continued inside. "It's important." He was moderately tall and slightly muscular, wearing the typical maroon sleeveless vest and full black pants. His black hair was nearly covered with his gray wolf-head hat. The ivory teeth of the wolf subtly gleamed in the light. The young man's eyes were dark brown and his skin a velvety brown with copper undertones. His aura felt deadly, and his veiny right hand never loosened its grip on his long black bow. He raised his thick black eyebrows waiting for Arka to acknowledge him.

"All right, Zay, no need to get impatient. Just wait outside, and I will be with you soon. Let me finish my breakfast."

Clenching his jaw, Zay didn't say a word. Instead, he adjusted the arrows in his quiver and huffed before walking out, slamming the door behind him. The loud echo buried the peaceful calm. The threatening atmosphere dissipated shortly afterward.

"I wonder what has him all fired up. I mean, Zay is always rude and demanding, but never early, rude, and demanding." Jai sighed as he went back to the kitchen to continue eating.

"Zay's had it hard, Jai. He's just trying to get by," Arka replied thoughtfully.

No harder than anyone else who has to live here.

"I know, but you offered him a place to stay and a steady job, and he turned it down. There's no point in complaining about it. Lower Ember is a tough place to live, but it's nobody else's problem if you turn down kindness and a good opportunity."

Arka hung his head as Jai spoke. Closing his eyes, he slowly shook his head.

"You don't understand. Zay has lived in survival mode all his life. It's all he knows—don't take chances, trust no one, stay alive or die."

"I guess you're right. He has had it rough. Well, I hope everything's okay." Jai knew all too well the hell that came with residing in Lower Ember. Even though things were trying for him and Arka, many Emberites, including Zay, had it worse. Honestly, they were all living in survival mode. While he'd always had the security of Arka as a father figure, Zay did not.

"I'm going to see what's got him heated. Go to the forge and light the fire. I'll be bringing the initial material for the fire daggers this morning. If you could make fifty blades a day that would be ideal—but no less than forty. I will talk to some of the youth and see if someone wants to learn to make the dagger handles with me. But I intend to pay Zay to work on the bombs."

"Of course, you have to choose the best man for the job. I'm going to eat some more eggs, get dressed, and start work. See you later," Jai replied, walking to the stove and refilling his plate.

After several minutes, he finished eating. Jai pulled his black pants and maroon sleeveless vest from the dark wooden clothes chest in his room. He quickly dressed and ran his fingers through his messy black hair as he headed to the forge. The area's sole purpose was for blacksmithing and was in Arka's backyard, about twenty feet from the house. They didn't have a big house; however, the yard was massive. Their forge was likened to a workshop with a fire pit in the center where Jai would do his blacksmithing. Arka preferred a larger area requiring a larger flame for his work since he specialized in shields and armor. Jai's specialty was swords and daggers; the work had made him quite strong and muscular. Jai lit the kiln and then began practicing his aim with the forging hammer and cross peen.

The old blacksmith forge was dimly lit, the only light coming from the flickering flames in the furnace. The air was thick with the acrid smell of burning coal, and the sound of the bellows pumping air into the fire filled the room. The walls were made of rough, weathered stone, and the floor was covered in a layer of black soot. Tools hung haphazardly from the walls, their edges glinting in the dim light. In the corner, a large anvil sat atop a heavy wooden stump, the surface scarred and dented from years of use. The forge was a place of rugged beauty, and despite the grime and soot that covered everything, there was an order to the chaos that spoke of years of practice and discipline.

Jai had waited in the forge for close to an hour and was getting anxious. It was true that Zay was quite rough around the edges and had a violent temper, but he hoped that no one was in trouble. However, trouble seemed to have a magnetic attraction to the forever-angry young man. A common concern in Lower Ember was to leave home and not make it back alive.

Sighing heavily, Jai began to work. He whistled a random tune as he heated the raw blocks of metal until they found their liquid form. The temperature of the forge rose; it was one of Jai's favorite parts about being in the workshop. Sweat began to bead on his forehead. He placed his face shield on as he used oversized tongs to pour the silver liquid into the molds. Hours passed, and Jai was in a rhythm of placing the heavy molds into the fire pit when he heard footsteps approaching.

Arka flung the door open and brushed everything off one of the work tables. "Bring him in here," he commanded. Uneasiness claimed Jai.

Something's happened.

Zay walked in carrying a body and laid it on the table. Jai stood in disbelief, "Zay, did you just kill a man?"

"No, Firefly, I took a shot at the enemy. I know it's hard for you to believe that I am capable of civic duty, but I am," Zay walked toward Jai in a hostile manner.

Jai hated being called Firefly. It was an affectionate term for a girl, reflecting that one was harmless and gentle. However, to call a man "Firefly" was a personal insult, insinuating that he is weak, spineless, and void of masculine energy. Jai squared his jaw in annoyance. He met Zay's energy and angrily marched up to him until they were standing face to face.

"Zay, enough," Arka reached into his pocket and paid him five gold coins. Zay smirked and patted Arka's back. Jai was shocked. That kind of money would set one nicely for the week.

Arka has gold?

"Thank you, Arka, the pleasure was mine." He turned to Jai, "Firefly, don't work too hard." Chuckling heartily, Zay turned, bumping his shoulder into Jai's as he left.

"Ugh, he's so irritating!" Jai looked at the body—a young man probably close to his age. His hair was blood red at the roots and dark brown as it neared the ends. Jai knew all too well why Zay shot him. After touching his hair, Jai confirmed it wasn't dyed. This man was from an enemy clan.

Arka's voice commanded Jai's attention.

"Zay will be back because he left his arrows in the quiver. I want you to prepare this body for cremation."

Jai nodded, but when his hand passed over the young man's rich brown face, he felt an unusual heat—heat that a dead man would not give off. Jai's hands began trembling. It was like they had a mind of their own.

Not this again.

"Arka, are you sure he's dead?" Jai was surprised at himself for asking.

"Yes, we checked the pulse," Arka absent-mindedly answered.

Jai checked the pulse, but there was none. The body was warm and radiating warmth. He held his breath. The presence of his gift was causing his body to tremble. It was like a wild animal breaking free from a cage. He placed his hand on the chest. Jai's hands felt like fire; something was off. It seemed like this man had just been killed. Even so, why would he be radiating this kind of heat?

He's not dead just yet. I can't let Arka know that.

"Jai!" Arka stormed toward him, "I said to prepare the body for cremation. Stop disgracing yourself by trying to examine a dead man. You're no doctor. Now get to it!" Arka punched Jai in the chest repeatedly.

"All right! I'm working on it! Don't worry. I've got it; you won't have to tell me again. Go ahead now, you don't want to be later than you already are to find us some help with this order," Jai smiled at Arka.

"This better be in progress when I return," Arka grumbled as he left the forge and headed to the house.

"Mhmm."

Once Arka was in the house, Jai nervously looked at his palms and back at the body. He found it odd that Arka wanted the man cremated in such a hurry. Then there was the element of the gold. Goosebumps raised all over his skin, and his stomach was jumpy. He took a breath to calm himself, "Okay, gift, it's no time to be temperamental. Let's see what you can do. Heavenly Stars, show me something." He closed his eyes and focused his palms over the heart. Jai felt a pulsing light radiate from his own hands. He kept his right hand over the heart and allowed his left hand to hover over the chest wound. No longer suppressing the sensation, he began to feel a sense of calm wash over him. To his astonishment, the wound started to heal within minutes.

"I never knew it could do that," he whispered.

Jai felt something approaching but was entirely consumed by the wonders of his gift. The sounds in the distance competed for his attention. But, being a novice, if he got distracted he'd lose his feeble grasp on his odd gift. The delicate golden-hued light emitted from his palms and illuminated the bloody wound. The blood quickly cleared, and the skin was rapidly knitting together, closing the wound. As it healed, the young man's eyes fluttered. They were a startling shade of amber! The young man began groaning.

Jai stopped. "You're alive," he whispered. His body trembled with excitement. He had never done that before. He was only acting on some unyielding sensation within him that urged him to let go—a power that refused to be bottled any longer.

The young man started to sit up, slowly propping himself up and resting on his elbows with his forearms. He looked at his body in disbelief, observed his surroundings, then his gaze met Jai. His amber orbs flitted around wildly, as his eyes traveled to the place of the fatal wound. The man's breath quickened, and he looked him in the eyes, "You-you, you're the Soul of the Sun. It's unbelievable. I was a dead man, but you—"

"Soul of what?"

"Soul of—"

His gaze suddenly peered past. Jai turned around slowly toward the forge door.

Ugh! Someone WAS approaching the forge!

He then remembered Arka's words, "Zay will be back because he left his arrows in the quiver."

"Oh, don't stop the show for me, you're both dead men now," Zay hissed, standing in the doorway. His aura was dark and foreboding, emanating an intense energy that seemed to vibrate with a sense of anger and malice. His eyes burned with a fierce intensity, conveying a deep-seated desire for blood and a willingness to do whatever it took to achieve it. Every muscle in his body seemed tense and coiled as if he was preparing for an imminent attack. His fists were clenched tightly, and his jaw was set in a firm line. As he stepped forward, his movements were sharp and deliberate, his body seeming to glide across the ground with a dangerous grace.

CHAPTER 2

Zay had a menacing look on his face and a deadly persona as he walked toward them.

Jai stood in front of the young man on the table, huffed, and clenched his fist. "He wasn't dead yet. I healed him," Jai tried to reason with Zay.

"That's crap! I killed him! I shot him straight in the chest—a death blow. I checked his pulse, and he was dead. Arka checked, and he was dead." He chuckled, "Maybe you're not a Firefly after all, but either way, you're a traitor. You got a gift! You should be exiled for that alone! But you used it to save a Pyrocean, the enemy. Those bastards kill your own people! Now you both die!"

Zay charged at Jai, who narrowly grabbed the cross peen he used for blacksmithing. Zay didn't have his arrows, for he had left them earlier. However, he used his longbow as a deadly weapon. The bow crashed into Jai's face, nearly cutting across his eye. An incredible archer, Zay was strong as he attacked, and Jai blocked with the hammer.

As they fought, Arka entered the forge. Looking at the former dead man alive and well, he quickly assessed the situation. He was in disbelief at the scene. He narrowed his eyes hissing at Jai, "JAI!!! You've ruined us!"

"Arka, please help me," Jai yelled, pleading for his assistance against a violent Zay.

Shaking his head, Arka's eyes narrowed as he reached into the back pocket of his black pants, "I should have killed you when I found you." He had a pocket knife in hand.

It became obvious to the young man on the table that Arka was not on Jai's side, and he blasted a punch laced with a brilliant orange fire at Arka. It was the least he could do to buy some time. He turned off the table and landed on his feet.

Arka ducked, narrowly avoiding the attack before steadying his stance and readying himself to fight. Jai put his hands up, letting light radiate from his left hand, and ignited a small, harmless fire in his right. The light blinded Zay, causing him to turn away. Utilizing the opportunity, Jai kicked him down by his knees. The fire in his right hand was gone!

Ugh this stupid, unstable ability!

Zay did a foot sweep, tripping Jai. He caught Jai's neck with the string of his bow and twisted it before pulling back, choking him. Gasping frantically, Jai gurgled and coughed, struggling to breathe. They were nearly even in terms of sheer strength, but Jai was severely disadvantaged against an experienced street fighter like Zay. He was elbowing Zay as much as he could but to no avail.

Seeing Jai struggling, the young man punched Arka in the chin using all his might, rendering him unconscious. Arka tumbled into the corner with the empty molds, his body laid motionless. The young man ran toward a choking Jai and kicked Zay square across the face, leaving him stunned and groaning, clutching his face.

"Let's go. We have to go now!" He dragged Jai up. Zay scurried to his feet and the man kicked a wild flame at his face. Zay jumped back as Jai crashed his foot into Zay's knee, causing the archer to fall straight back, hitting his head on the forge floor.

Jai was shaken and struggling to catch his breath, "What?" His now golden-colored eyes wandered about the room.

"Let's go!" The young man violently dragged Jai away from the forge just as Arka began to stir. They ran through the town. "The old man won't be knocked out for long. The archer is relentless. I didn't want to kill anyone, so we have to keep moving," the young man huffed as he led Jai through the city streets of Lower Ember.

Within minutes, Zay and Arka were behind them at a great distance. Arka had peeled off—his age didn't allow him to keep up the pursuit. But Zay, he was like a wild man. It was like he hadn't been in a fight at all. He was going strong, pressing forward with ninja-like speed. And he was gaining on them.

The young man looked back, "Man, he's strong and fast. He killed me once. I don't wanna die twice on the same day. Let's turn here."

It was a wooded area past the town and was highly undeveloped. Most Emberites who came here were big-game hunters who could handle the terrain. Something that Jai, the blacksmith, was not. Knowing he didn't have much choice, either fight Zay or follow the stranger, Jai chose the wiser and followed the amber-eyed man into the unkept forest. They stayed quiet as they moved as quickly as they could through the thick brush.

They hid in a moderately thick area surrounded by bushes and vine-covered shrubs. Raising his hand near Jai's face, the man motioned for Jai to stay quiet. He crouched low in the thick brush of the forest, his breaths coming in short gasps as he tried to steady his racing heart. He dared not move, not even an inch, not wanting any sudden rustling to give away his position.

Zay caught up shortly after. "All right now, come on out!" Jai peeped between the brush and saw Zay, his lower lip busted and swollen. Consumed by rage, he was wildly swinging his bow high and low, swiping at the brush, trying to find them.

"Come on now, I don't have all day. Jai, I won't hurt you. I'll let Arka decide your fate! Isn't that what you wanted, Firefly? I'll let him decide your fate." Zay walked closer to where they were hiding. He yelled a feral yell and tugged at his hair. He violently tossed his bow down before falling to his knees. "Come on, I haven't eaten in days. I'm just trying to get paid, man. Don't make this harder on me. I-I just wanna eat without having to steal."

Zay looked around; there was complete silence. Even the creatures of the woods denied his existence and stayed silent. He sighed and plopped to the ground, about three feet from where Jai and the young man were hiding. Jai held his breath, not wanting his nerves to give him away. His heart was pounding; he dared not move or breathe.

"Great hell, that guy must have been some game hunter to get through that. I'm starving. Well, maybe Arka will let me eat something after I return these coins to him. I'll just have to report this to Agni and somehow survive." Zay stood, secured his bow and wolf hat, then left in a huff. Jai watched him go. Only once he completely cleared the woods did Jai take a deep breath. His entire body went limp.

"Thanks for saving me," the young man said, still lying on his back.

"Mhmm. What's your name?"

"Arrow. I guess you're Jai. Your power is amazing. I never thought I'd live to meet a Legend." Arrow stood and began walking deeper into the forest. Jai followed him.

A what? What the heck is a Legend?

"What do you mean, a Legend?"

Arrow stopped dead in his tracks, "You don't know who you are? I mean, maybe you call it something else. My people would call you the Soul of the Sun."

Jai continued to gaze at Arrow, his eyebrows wrinkled with confusion.

Arrow's eyes widened, "Have you seen your eyes?"

"Yeah, I look at them every day. What kind of question is that? What does that have to do with Legends?" Jai rolled his eyes.

"Jai, you're a Legend . . . a golden-eyed Legend . . . a Fireheart Legend."

Jai's expression was blank. Maybe Arrow was just tired. "You're saying that like it's supposed to mean something to me," Jai scoffed.

Arrow glared at him with a serious expression, using his body to block Jai's way, "You're what the Firehearts have been waiting hundreds of years for! Look, just come on this way."

"Why would I trust you? My life was going just fine until you showed up."

"It was? I couldn't tell. That Zay looked like he's been waiting all of his life to kill you. Arka said he should have killed you when he found you. You've been living in a shack, and you work like a slave. If I didn't know that you were a blacksmith, I'd have never thought your pants were actually supposed to be dark red." Arrow pointed to Jai's heavily calloused hands and ragtag clothes.

"It's called a struggle." Jai bristled up; his anger was slowly rising.

"Look, you saved my life. I saved yours. At this moment, between the people you know and me, I'm not going to kill you. But we both know that they will. I've got a place to stay. You can either go back to where hell awaits or come with me."

Jai remained quiet as he watched Arrow's back disappear among the trees. Looking back toward the heart of Lower Ember, his heart twisted at the thought of leaving. It wasn't perfect, but it was a part of him. It was his home.

However, he knew Arrow was right. In the blink of an eye, his life in Lower Ember was in the past. A death warrant hung over his head if he returned. After a silent goodbye, he hurried to follow Arrow. The pair walked for nearly an hour in silence. Eventually, they made their way to a small, wooden makeshift house well camouflaged with leaves and branches. Arrow looked at Jai, "We'll be safe here for a while." He showed Jai the corner with blankets rolled up and stacked and a bag of dried meat and fruits. There were also several jugs of water lined up along another wall.

"Seems like you try to be prepared," Jai mumbled.

Arrow nodded as he walked to the corner to get two blankets. He handed one to Jai, unrolled one for himself, and sat down with some dried meat. Jai repeated Arrow's actions and unrolled his blanket. Arrow offered him some dried meat. Jai just looked at it. "What's wrong? It's just wrapped tight in salt to preserve the meat. It's still good. Here, I keep some red pepper flakes on me all the time. Try it."

Reluctantly he accepted the food. "Thanks, I was just thinking about Zay—how he hadn't eaten in days."

"Sorry. I can't show much sympathy to my former murderer." Arrow continued, "So, what else can you do?"

Jai ignored the comment about murder to suppress the impulse to ask Arrow what reason Zay would have to kill him. Then he reminded himself, this was Zay. Violence was his answer to just about anything. He didn't need a reason, that was just who he had grown to be. Focusing on Arrow's question, he replied, "What do you mean?"

"You don't have to be modest. I saw you do that thing with the light; then you turned light into fire. What else can you do?"

"That's it besides healing, but you weren't awake for that. I just learned that I could heal wounds; that had never happened before. The fire is temperamental. I can always generate light, but when I do, it changes my eye color. I had never shown anyone my gifts before."

"Why not? A lot of people for many generations have been waiting for you. Jai, you're that answer to a lot of people's prayers."

"Why not? Did you not just see what happened back there? I can't just go around showing everyone that I'm gifted! It makes me a target! Most people in Lower Ember lost their gifts after the civil war with Upper Ember, or they were born giftless. I haven't met anyone there who is gifted other than myself."

"Lost their gifts?"

"Yeah, the war broke my people's spirits. It's rare to find someone who believes in the Universe, at least in Lower

Ember. When you lose your connection to the Universe, it is common for the Universe to remove your gift."

"Lose your connection to the Universe? So what do you believe?"

"Based on the norm, I'll be lucky to live until fifty. If this gift will help me live long enough to find some answers, I'll protect it for as long as it protects me. If believing in the Universe will secure the gift, I'll believe."

"You don't have to live like this. Living to fifty is not a life! You can do better than settle for that. Like I said, you're the answer to our people's prayers."

"Why me? Why not you? Look at yourself, you're a hunter. You're a true Fireheart. What makes me special? What makes me destined and not you? What do I have that you don't—or anyone else?"

Arrow pointed to Jai's face, "Golden eyes, you have what none of us can ever have. You have the sign of the rebirth of the four Legends. The birth of a golden-eyed child signals a trigger for an era of Legends. Only one person every so many hundreds of years can have golden eyes. And they are right there, sitting in your eye sockets. The Universe chose you, Jai. For Firehearts, our eyes are light brown, honey brown, or amber, and hazel is rare and reserved for lightning abilities. But gold, only a Fireheart Legend can have gold eyes. . . . Wow, I sounded like my father just now."

"But my eyes aren't gold all the time. I mean, this may not even be 'gold.' It's probably just a very light brown. See? They change color when I use my gift, but then they always return to brown."

"Jai, your eyes are still gold. I'm looking at them," Arrow replied, shaking his head.

"What!? That's not possible. That's not normal. I'm telling you that's not normal! They have never changed for that long."

"The Universe knows best. Those guys back there are supporting the World Order. That's probably why Zay killed me."

"Or because you have the blood of an enemy clan. Looking at your hair, are you half Pyrocean?"

Arrow squared his jaw in annoyance, "No! I'm just Pyrocean—father Pyrocean, mother Pyrocean!"

"Yeah, I didn't mean to offend you," Jai replied.

"No, it just gets annoying. I know you didn't mean anything. . . . So do you support the World Order?"

"No, the idea of going against the Universe unsettles me, and I don't want to lose my gift. I am just careful not to irritate Arka since he is completely against the Universal Order. I don't know what happened to him, but he was once gifted. He lost his gift after he returned from the civil war. When I was young, I was separated from my family. Arka found me and raised me. The first few nights, I would dream about my father teaching me of the Universe and its blessings. I know Arka doesn't believe, but he gave me a home and love and called me his son. I have frequent dreams about my past that I can never remember once I wake up. I can't remember any details about my childhood. I just remember the day I got separated and Arka found me."

"You don't remember your family?"

"No. I remember the sound of my father's voice, and that's all. I don't even remember what my mother looks like. If I were to see her, I'd never recognize her."

"Man, that's tough. I suppose you can say I'm separated from my family as well. I know it's not easy. I realize that we just met, and this is not an ideal situation, but just hear me out. You can't go back there. Your eyes have changed, and in your town, you're going to be targeted until they eventually kill you. I hate to say it, but that chapter in your life is over. I can help you out, but of course, you are not obligated to do anything."

If he wanted to kill me, he would have already done it. His gift is stronger than mine by a long shot. And . . . he's right. I can't go back there. Not like this.

"I am a member of the Flamethrowers. We are an arching organization founded as your predecessor's personal military."

"My predecessor?"

"Yeah, Cyra of Kindle, so basically, since you are her successor, the Flamethrowers are technically your military now, but I'll have to talk over the details with Calida."

Cyra of Kindle?

Jai's skin was covered in goosebumps as he heard the name Cyra. He had never heard that name before. "Who's Calida?"

"The leader of the Flamethrowers. Her grandfather served under Cyra."

"Whoa, are you sure I'm the Golden-Eyed Legend?"

"I wish I had a mirror to show you that your eyes are still gold," Arrow sighed. "Rest up. I'll keep watch on the hut." Arrow stood up and walked outside.

It seems like I annoyed him. That wasn't my intention.

Jai finished his dried meat and lay on the blanket. His mind was swirling with thoughts of Arka, Zay, and Arrow. He would have never thought Arka would try to kill him. Zay hated the world, so that wasn't unbelievable coming from him. But Arka was like a father to him. And a part of him missed Arka, even after seeing hatred that spewed from his eyes. He was in his sixties, a hard-working and usually mild-tempered man. Jai remembered his dark honey-brown eyes, how they would gaze upon him with love and care. But today, those eyes looked at him with disgust. The memory chilled him to the bone. He just would have never believed that Arka would do anything to take anyone's life.

Jai thought about what Zay said. He hadn't eaten in days. He was willing to pay Arka back just to get a meal. Jai felt for him, such was the struggle. How did Arka get that gold? Even when business was at its peak, they struggled to make ends meet. If they got a few silver coins, that was considered being paid exceedingly well. But gold? What kind of job did Zay have that required killing? Zay killed Arrow and was more than eager to kill again. Arrow seemed like a good person, but they just met. Was being

Pyrocean the only reason Zay killed him, or was there something else?

Moments passed and Jai could feel tension pulling at his temples. He was exhausted from overthinking. Breathing slowly, he settled his thoughts, deciding to focus on the Universe. The Universe gifted him. He didn't understand his gift, but he was thankful to have it.

Is this what it means to have a purpose? Is this destiny? I've always believed in the power of the Stars. Why not? I'm not dead yet. I've always had some sort of a home, a rare luxury in Lower Ember. Maybe the Universe really is with me. Thinking back on it, my life has been easier than most in my town. I don't have anything to lose by going with Arrow. Maybe... I have everything to gain.

CHAPTER 3

The night had reached its peak before Arrow returned inside. He was surprised to see Jai awake and waiting for him. "It felt kinda strange to rest during the day," Jai remarked.

"Well, I just thought it was a lot for you to take in, so a little rest and solitude would do you good. If you so choose, you've got a journey ahead of you. You'd be no good wound up," Arrow explained. "We're going to leave soon and get to the thick inner part of these woods."

"Um, not even the best game hunters go that far," Jai whispered, immediately feeling distrust toward Arrow.

That sounds like the perfect place to try and kill someone.

"That's the point, to not be found," Arrow replied.

"So that's it? We live our life trying to not be found?"

"No, the Flamethrowers aren't hiding, we're preparing," Arrow rolled his eyes playfully. "After Cyra passed, the Firehearts fell apart. Actually, to be quite fair, the last four Legends did a greater disservice than anything. Well, except Basir, the Windmasters made progress." Arrow stood up and moved everything back to its respective corner.

Basir?

Jai stood up as well and began helping him tidy the hut. "How do you know all of this stuff?"

Arrow stopped in his tracks. His body tensed and his fists clenched. He sighed, "My father." He averted Jai's gaze.

Jai noticed that Arrow seemed uncomfortable talking about his family, so he decided to let it go. Once the hut was tidy, they left. Arrow led Jai away and into the depths of the woods. It was challenging to walk in the thick of the woods. There was barely a difference between dark green and black. As the night sky rose and they walked through the forest, the only sound that broke the eerie silence was the crunching of fallen leaves and twigs under their feet. The moon, shrouded by clouds, provided little illumination, making the already dense forest seem even more foreboding.

There were creatures overhead and crawling around, and Jai was tripping over something every other step. Arrow was a few paces ahead moving with complete ease. He stayed close, struggling to keep Arrow in view. He did not want to get lost. It was difficult enough during full daylight, but the night was different. Jai could barely see what was ahead of him.

"You know, everything in the woods is afraid of fire, even the trees. So don't worry," Arrow spoke without looking at Jai, expertly navigating the forest.

He must have sensed my apprehension.

Jai took a breath and calmed down. He had heard many rumors about the Pyroceans. Some say they are half-dragon, others say they are like animals and can smell fear. But it was a well-known fact that the Pyroceans had the best army in the world. Half beast or not, it didn't matter when you had enough power to make the world bend a knee. There was something about Arrow that he liked. He was mysterious, but he was free. And that freedom was something Jai only imagined having. What kind of life could he have enjoyed if he wasn't desperately hiding his powers? He couldn't fathom what it was like to not be a slave to your situation.

"I can't always get fire. It's temperamental. I can always use light and heal, but that fire is something else. Whenever I do get fire, it's like lighting a stupid matchstick. If I lose focus on it, even for a second, it's gone. Are my eyes still gold?"

"Yeah, since the moment you healed me and I opened my eyes, your eyes have been gold," Arrow reassured him. "Hey, look," Arrow stopped in his tracks, "Do you believe me?"

"I don't know what to believe; everyone I've known wants me dead. I just revived a dead man for let's see... the first time in my life! I mean, if someone told you they could bring the dead back to life, would you believe them? I don't think so! All I know is I don't want to die. Since I don't want to die, what you're giving me is all I've got."

Arrow turned around and smiled, "I'm Pyrocean, I get it! The first time I came to these parts, people were shocked over abilities that are common where I'm from. Maybe this journey will answer a lot of questions you have about yourself. Since when does fire heal? That's a Waterbearer trait. Isn't something that incredible worth exploring? I am not forcing you into anything. I just want to help. As I said, I'm technically sworn to your service. Let's go. It's not much farther." The pair continued for another ten minutes into the thick woods where a giant tree stood. The trunk was at least twenty feet wide. It was probably the tallest tree in the woods.

"Behind here," Arrow motioned for Jai to come. As they approached a clearing, there was a large cabin. Jai was in awe because it was so well camouflaged. In the darkness of night, it was nearly invisible. The cabin could pass for scenery if one was not looking at it closely. The thick layers of moss and lichen covered its wooden exterior, blending it seamlessly into the surrounding foliage. It looked like a natural extension of the forest as if it had been there for centuries. Although it seemed abandoned, Jai felt something strangely inviting. He could see faint glimpses of flickering light coming from one of the cabin's moss-shrouded windows.

The light was faint, but it illuminated the surrounding area just enough to reveal the intricate patterns of the moss and lichen that covered the cabin. One could see tendrils of greenery creeping up the walls and encircling the door handle. It was as if the cabin was alive and had become one with the forest.

Arrow knocked on the door. Jai noticed that the knock was unique, but as quickly as he heard it, he forgot. The door cracked open. Arrow motioned for him to come closer, and he pushed the door, allowing Jai and himself to go inside.

Jai was greatly surprised to see at least a dozen people looking at him when he walked through the door. Immediately feeling uneasy, he readied himself to fight. A quiet rage ignited inside of him, his hand traveled to his belt, but he didn't have his hammer.

The first thing that caught his eye was the wine-red rugs that adorned the wooden floors. Their deep hues added warmth to the space and gave off an inviting feel. The walls were lined with various types of bows and arrows, each one carefully mounted on display. A stone fireplace dominated one corner of the space. The flames danced and flickered, casting a warm glow that illuminated the entire space. Above it, a mantle displayed an array of antlers. A crumbling bookshelf filled with tattered books stood in one corner of the room. Jai turned his head and observed the kitchen area. It was simple but functional with a wooden table; however, there were no chairs. Relaxing his arms slowly, he acknowledged his new reality.

I'm not in the forge anymore.

"Don't stare. That's rude," Arrow scolded them, and they all looked away. "Don't mind them. None of us have seen golden eyes before," he chuckled before leading him through the cabin past everyone's murmurs. In the far back was a woman who had her back turned to them. She was looking at a particular map on the wall. There were land masses of distinctly different shapes and sizes. He could make out the name Wyndhm; the place was unfamiliar to Jai.

"Cal, do you have a minute?" Arrow gently touched her shoulder.

She didn't turn around, "Sure, what's up?"

Jai was taken aback when he heard the power in her voice. It was assertive and firm.

Arrow smiled, "Why don't you take a look?" She turned around, and her honey-colored eyes went wide as her jaw dropped. "Cal, you shouldn't stare. That's rude." She quickly closed her mouth and cleared her throat.

"Right! I'm sorry. I didn't mean to stare, but your eyes. I never imagined this. The gold is so intense yet gentle. I'm

Calida, leader of the Flamethrowers." She walked toward him, touching his face in awe.

"I'm Jai," he replied. He took a step back to put some distance between them. Calida blinked awkwardly upon realizing that she had gotten carried away. She quickly placed her hands at her side and took a small step back.

Arrow patted Jai's shoulder, "The three of us should talk in private."

"I can manage that." Calida walked to the center of the cabin, "Everyone, hear me! I am going to send everyone out on a training assignment."

"In the middle of the night?" someone whispered.

"Yes, you will be going on a hunt. I want one precise shot to a vital area of your game. You have one hour. This will allow us to restock some of our essentials. Do your best. We all can see that we are one step closer to fulfilling our mission. Now take your positions."

Everyone scurried to make one single file line. Calida began counting. She counted heads up to fifteen. "Number one and number twelve, stay back and guard the cabin. You will use crossbows. Odd numbers grab longbows, and even numbers grab recurve bows. Your hour starts now." There was one cabin wall filled from top to bottom with bow and arrow slots, and everyone rushed to the wall to get what they needed.

Is she a general of something? She talks like she's commanding soldiers.

Jai observed her body language. Her hands rested on her hips. Her stance was wide, back straight, and chin pointed up. Power exuded from her. Jai was impressed.

After about five minutes, everyone was outside, leaving Arrow, Calida, and Jai. Feeling more relaxed, he took in her features. Calida was beautiful. Her hair was off-black and pulled into a ponytail with a few stray wavy strands falling in front of her face. Her eyes were honey-colored, and her skin was light brown with deep golden undertones. She had a scar running in a straight line from under her right eye to her jaw. It had healed but left a mark. The delicate light from the fireplace only accentuated her features. Jai was still in awe that she sent the others hunting in the thick of night. He carefully watched the movement of her eyes. She crossed her arms in front of her while waiting for someone to speak.

"So, are you going to talk to me or what?" Calida asked in a temper.

"Well, you're the leader, so I thought you were going to start," Arrow shrugged his shoulders.

"Hello! You brought him here, Mr. Second-in-command, so get to it!"

"Miss Calida, leader of the Flamethrowers, you can clearly see you're in front of a legend, so go for the formal introduction," Arrow retorted.

She tilted her head, and her eyes widened in annoyance.

Jai rolled his eyes and interrupted their nonsense. "Are you two done?" Jai asked the bickering pair. "I'm Jai, nineteen years old, and an Emberite. My gifts include light manipulation and healing; fire is temperamental. Lower Ember is against the Universal Order, and the man who raised me wants me dead. I can't remember anything about my early upbringing since I'm an amnesiac. Anything else?"

Calida and Arrow were silent for several moments.

"I'm sorry. Arrow and I tend to get worked up sometimes. You have amnesia?"

"Yeah, I can't remember my childhood. If I push myself to try and remember, I'll start forgetting other things. It used to be worse, but I have a handle on it."

"I'm sorry, Jai." She was quiet for a moment. "Your gifts of light manipulation and healing are unique. You may be the first Fireheart to have that ability. Like Arrow said, you are clearly the Fireheart Legend. And the timeline is about right too," she looked towards Arrow.

"It is usually about two to three hundred years from the death of the last Legend to the birth of the new one. My grandfather, Horus of Ember, served under your predecessor, Cyra of Kindle. She developed a small personal army of archers and acolytes to serve as her guard. Once she passed, my grandfather decided that we should keep the tradition. Generations of Flamethrowers have lived, trained, and died waiting to be of service to the next golden-eyed Legend."

"The world has fallen into such disorder that we need the Legend to set us straight," Arrow chimed in.

"Are we talking about the wars?" Jai asked.

"Yes," Arrow replied.

"What does that have to do with me?"

"Where's your team?" Calida asked.

"Team? What are you talking about?" Jai asked.

"Team, squad, alliance, band?" Calida asked.

"What?" Jai looked at her in utter confusion.

"So the One Who Knows hasn't sought you out," Arrow asked in disbelief.

"The what?"

"Obviously not yet, but remember, Cyra didn't meet her fellow Legends until they were in their thirties. So, that's not unreasonable." Calida explained.

"Yeah but Basir met Ila when they were teenagers."

Calida sighed, "Well obviously, Jai has not met any other Legend!"

"What are you talking about? Who are these Legends and what are they for? Why is this even important?" Jai asked.

"The prior Legends were Cyra, Basir, Aenon, and Ila. Cyra was the Fireheart, Basir a Windmaster, Aenon a Beach Waterbearer, and Ila a Landkeeper. These Legends are gifts from the Universe, and their lives are lessons to the people they represent. In the past, some Legends taught us new abilities, like lightning for Firehearts or ice for Waterbearers. Sometimes they are to lead us through a hard time or solve our problems. And sometimes, they challenge us so that we will be ready to face an obstacle that we cannot see coming. At the end of the day, Legends have to define their purpose and forge their legacy."

"Jai, we are here to help, serve, and protect you. All of us are willing to die for your success. So please accept us. We are a gift from Cyra to you." Calida gently touched his shoulder.

Jai closed his eyes. In less than twenty-four hours, his life had changed.

Is this my purpose? What will they think once they realize that I'm not powerful? It's life or death for me at this point.

"I accept you. Arka raised me, but I never believed in the World Order for fear of losing my gift. I want to understand it better, my gift. I never want to lie or appear as something that I'm not. I don't feel strong enough to handle my own gift right now, so I don't know if I can solve the problems of the Firehearts. There isn't anything I can do to end a war," Jai looked down at his lap.

"Your gift is like a muscle. It gets stronger with use. What you don't use, you lose. You just need some training, that's all," Calida assured him.

"Where can I train? Who will train me?"

"We can probably handle training—"

"No, Arrow, he needs the best, and you know what I mean," Calida cut Arrow off mid-sentence. Arrow shook his head and furrowed his brows. Calida continued speaking, "It's either Tora or Sheraga."

Jai had no idea who she was talking about.

"Tora won't take him. He has enough he's dealing with. Besides, it would require more physical danger to Jai to get him there. We would have to pass through Ember to get to Kindle," Arrow grumbled.

"So Sheraga it is," Calida sighed.

"Who's Sheraga?"

Arrow put his hand over Calida's mouth, "The DragonLord of Pyroc."

"Hey, that's where you're from. Let's go there," Jai smiled.

Annoyed, Calida pulled her face away from Arrow's hand. "Okay, I'll brief the Flamethrowers. They should be heading back soon. Jai, feel free to get to know them when they come back. They are going to be excited to get to know you too."

"If you need anything, let us know," Arrow sighed and stood to leave.

"Arrow doesn't seem to like talking about his family or Pyroc. I can push myself to learn another way if that is better for everyone."

"We made an oath to help, serve, and protect you. Don't worry about Arrow . . . I've got him. Over there, to your left, is a washroom. You can wash up there. You will see a closet with some extra towels. You can use one. To your right, that big room is where we all sleep. Then there's another washroom to the left of that room. We cook, eat, and socialize, usually sitting on those large maroon rugs. Now, we are Firehearts, it can get a bit wild in here. Just make yourself at home." Calida smiled and stood up, following Arrow. Jai smiled. They seemed so close that he felt a warm feeling in his chest. He hadn't had friends before. Zay was probably the closest person he had to a friend, and Zay really wasn't his friend. He stood up and went to wash up as Calida told him to feel free to do.

Once Jai closed the door, Calida gently brushed Arrow's shoulder, "It's going to be okay."

"I'm sorry I got upset; it's just I hate that place. I know you're right. Jai needs to go there and have the space and freedom to learn. And everyone knows Sheraga is an incredible teacher," Arrow sighed.

"I wasn't accepted then, and I will probably be accepted less now. So much has happened. I know this isn't about me and that we have to put what Jai needs first. I just swore to the Stars that I'd never go back there. That I'd never be that person again." He brushed loose waves of Pyrocean hair away from his amber eyes.

"I know a lot has happened, and there's a lot of pain involved with going back. But it is still your family. All families experience things like this, but it doesn't mean that the love is gone. Arrow, your family loves you, and I'll be there. And it's just going to be temporary. So let my presence make a difference. You always told me we're stronger together, so let's be strong together." They took a deep breath. Arrow turned and held her, his chin on her head, lingering in her embrace.

CHAPTER 4

"Calida, Arrow, the archers are in sight." A voice came from behind the door. Arrow let Calida go.

"Thank you, Alena. You and Cahya come on in," Arrow instructed. The young woman, Alena, and the young man, Cahya, returned their crossbows to their proper slot on the wall. As they turned around, they were stopped by Calida.

"Jai is washing up. Spend some time with him. Help him mingle and get to know the Flamethrowers." They nodded and sat on the heavily worn maroon rug. The other Flamethrowers began to line up their game outside before standing directly in front of it.

"I'll do the head count and check the game," Calida went outside. The dark of night swallowed her figure as she walked.

Jai came out of the washroom with his hair slightly damp and his face freshly washed. He looked around. Arrow was looking outside the door. Before he could walk over to him, he heard someone call his name.

"Jai, come sit with us," Cahya motioned for him. Reluctant at first, Jai walked over and sat on the rug with them. "I'm Cahya, and this is Alena. We're glad to be of service to you."

"Mhmm."

Cahya didn't seem fazed by Jai's lack of enthusiasm. "Did my sister teach you the Flamethrower knock?"

"Your sister?"

"Yeah, Calida," Cahya replied. Now that he said something, Jai could see the resemblance. The siblings had similar light brown skin tones, small noses, and almond-shaped, honey-colored eyes. He turned to Alena. His eyes widened as she smiled at him. Her skin was smooth and golden brown, and her eyes were a pretty light brown. Her delicate lips were full, and she had a dimple on her left cheek when she smiled. It perfectly complimented her heart-shaped face.

Suddenly, he remembered that Cahya had asked him a question. "No, what's the knock?" Jai eventually replied.

"The normal knock is like a heartbeat. One-two . . . one-two . . . one-two. An emergency is the same beat but faster, one-two, one-two, one-two. A crisis code is the phrase, 'Did you know that only a Legend can have golden eyes?' " Alena explained to him.

"Come to think of it, Arrow did do that heartbeat knock when we were outside," Jai reflected. The rest of the Flamethrowers started coming inside and returning their bows and arrows to the wall. Then some went to the washroom, others went to the sleeping room, while the rest sat down socializing.

"What is a crisis code for?"

"The past generations of Flamethrowers were outcasts due to their alliance with Cyra of Kindle. Sometimes, we're targeted. If an enemy makes it this far, we hear the crisis code and immediately ready our weapons for attack," Cahya explained.

Targeted due to their alliance? What did this woman do?

"Arin, come here," Alena called. Arin sat beside Alena, looking like her clone. It became evident that they were twins.

"I'm Jai. Nice to meet you."

"Nice to meet you too," Arin smiled at him with her dimpled right cheek.

Wow, she has a beautiful smile.

They looked identical; however, Arin exuded a certain joyfulness. It made him smile. When Arin slowly averted her gaze from his, Jai felt a slight flush cross his cheeks. But he was thankful that Cahya and Alena did not seem to notice.

Calida walked over, standing tall with her shoulders back and her chin held high. Her gaze was focused and unwavering as her arms stayed at her sides. Her legs were firmly planted; she looked grounded and unshakable. Her body language inspired respect and immediately quieted the Flamethrowers.

"Everyone, hear me!" Calida began to speak, "We all have recognized that the Legend has graced us with his presence. For that, we are thankful. It is time to fulfill our oath to help, serve, and protect him. Jai is learning his role as well as us. While we are learning how to best fulfill our roles, we will treat one another with respect. Your brother's honor, your sister's honor, is your own! We are a military organization. There is no room for internal issues. We work together as one. I know everyone is fired up with anticipation of our next steps. Arrow will explain those details." She motioned for Arrow to come and speak.

"All right, Calida and I have chosen a team to accompany Jai to Pyroc for training."

"Pyroc?"

"Training?"

"He needs training; it's just like Cyra."

"I mean look at him, he's probably a teenager."

"So are we! Gifts are supposed to come naturally."

"Look at his clothes, he's probably from Lower Ember. Don't they kill you if you have a gift or something?"

Jai could hear the puzzled buzz among the Flamethrowers when training was mentioned. He didn't like being compared to Cyra. He had only heard negative things about her. Was it unusual to not be able to handle your gift at his age?

Arrow cleared his throat, and the room fell silent. "This team will be led by Calida and include Cahya, Alena, Arin, and me. Dysis, your post will be to secure all messages from the cabin to Cahya in Pyroc. Suvan, you will hold my post until I return and channel all messages to Dysis. Everyone else will complete their usual duties under the guidance of Kiran and Yuuna. We have decided that Yuuna will act as leader in Calida's absence. Everyone will respect her leadership and follow her orders as you would Calida. If there are any questions, meet me in the hut before sunrise in the morning." Arrow clapped his hands and started to leave.

Arrow's gaze met Jai's. "Hey, I want you to feel at home here, but I'll be at the hut if you need anything. If you'd rather sleep there, that's fine too," Arrow smiled and left.

"Hello Jai, I'm Dysis," a short, petite young woman said, walking toward the group. Her skin was rich and deep brown with warm undertones, and her eyes were a striking hazel. Behind that piercing gaze was an aura of friendliness. It was amazing how pretty the women were.

"Dysis, let's look over this route real quick! Hey Jai, I'm Suvan," the young man called for Dysis and waved at Jai with a twinkle in his honey-colored eyes.

"So, are you excited?" Arin asked with her dimple showing on her right cheek. She lightly touched his shoulder.

"Actually, I am. I've never been outside of Lower Ember. I had to work for food and to keep a roof over my head, so I never had time to explore. I have rarely used my gift because my father figure was with the World Order," Jai explained.

"Oh, I'm sorry to hear life was like that. Though, it's surprising that you say you rarely used your gift. You look so strong," she lowered her eyes.

Is she blushing?

Jai chuckled, "I'm a blacksmith, can't have scrawny arms doing that!"

She covered her mouth as she giggled, "I guess not. I'm sure you're going to love Pyroc. It is nice and hot, and your skin will get addicted to the heat from the volcanoes. It's a wonderful place to learn how to use your gift," Arin said excitedly. The love for Pyroc was evident as he listened to every word that fell from her lips.

"I'm excited to learn more about my gift and how to be useful to the Firehearts," Jai nodded. "What are some things the Flamethrowers can do?"

"Well, all of us are master archers. We also 'throw flames.' It's a technique where your fire goes from your fingertips to the arrowhead without burning the entire arrow. Our great-grandfather developed that technique," Cahya beamed with pride.

"Arin and I have a special heat-sensing technique that we do. Our father is from Kindle, and that's a signature technique from that area," Alena chimed.

"What does that do?"

"It allows you to use your fire gift to see things without using your eyes. You feel the shape of a thing by the heat it gives off. Your eyes then visualize it as colors. Warm colors for living things or hot things. Cooler colors show non-living, or cold things." Arin explained.

"I didn't know that Firehearts could possess these different gifts. They are all so unique," Jai wondered.

"The terms for it are subtypes or supplementary abilities. Do you want to know what's unique? Dysis, she was born with the rare hazel eyes," Cahya whispered.

"What does that mean?" Jai whispered.

"Her parents were lightning masters," Cahya replied.

"Arrow told me about hazel being a rare eye color; it's only for lightning, right?"

"When people have hazel eyes, they cannot use a flame in its normal form, and they can only use the advanced forms of fire. Hazel is the eye color of the lightning ability, but Dysis has a lightning and laser ability. She was born with only lightning and learned to generate heat lasers right from her fingers. She's incredible," Cahya said in awe. His cheeks flushed every time he said Dysis' name.

"I wonder what produces the different eye colors in Firehearts," Jai wondered.

"If you want to know anything about the history of Firehearts and Fireheart abilities, ask Arrow. You know, his family—" Alena was cut off by Cahya's hand.

"Alena! You know Arrow hates people bringing that up! And my sister would skin me alive if she thought we were talking about that. Jai, if you want to know, just ask Arrow. He's brilliant and knows a lot about Firehearts," Cahya summarized, cutting his eyes at Alena, who mumbled something.

Suvan and Dysis came over to sit with them, "Whoa, your eyes are like little suns on your face," Suvan exclaimed. Jai wasn't sure if he was excited or not, but Suvan had a very loud, booming voice. It wasn't really deep, but it was very loud.

Dysis rolled her eyes at Suvan, who playfully pushed her with his tawny muscular arm. "Little suns, was that the best you could do?" Cahya looked like he had stopped breathing once Dysis sat beside him.

"Come on, Dysis, like you could do better! Where are you from, Jai?"

"I'm from Ember, Lower Ember," Jai replied.

"I'm from Ember too, the upper part. What's your gift like?"

"It's light manipulation. I can generate light from my hands, and I can use the light for healing purposes too. The part I'm trying to get better at is turning light into fire," Jai shared.

"Wow, of all the gifts, I've never heard of that one . . . ever," Dysis whispered.

The rest of the Flamethrowers looked at each other in disbelief. Suvan leaned closer to Jai. His eyes were twinkling with curiosity, "Can you show us?"

"Yeah!" The rest chimed in.

"I'll show you a small light. The bigger it is, the more it is blinding, except to me, of course," Jai opened his hands and revealed a pure light, golden in hue. Glowing fleck-like particles slowly moved about in his hand. Jai immediately relaxed at the warm sensation. It reflected the beauty of the sun, its strength, and its gentleness all at once. Seeing how the Flamethrowers were nearly mesmerized, Jai began to dim the light until it disappeared. Suvan was the first to look at him.

"That was amazing," he slapped him on the back hard enough to rearrange his internal organs. Jai nearly jumped as Suvan continued talking as if he didn't nearly knock the wind out of him. "I've never seen a gift like that before." The rest of them were still staring at his empty hand. Suvan looked at them and turned to Jai, "Don't worry, they're struck."

"What?"

"It's what I do with my gift; the element's intensity nearly hypnotizes those watching. I just have fire, but it's the same thing. Did you know that only Firehearts and Waterbearers can use their gifts for hypnosis?" Suvan asked.

"No, I didn't," Jai rubbed the back of his head. He wasn't sure how to feel about his abilities being compared to the natural enemies of the Firehearts, the Waterbearers.

After a few minutes, Cahya, Alena, Arin, and Dysis began looking around.

"Whoa, now that was something," Cahya exclaimed.

"Another Legend that has a new ability," Arin chimed to Alena, who nodded in excitement.

"Jai," Calida said, "you need some rest. You'll find sleeping hard in Pyroc, so you must rest."

"If Sheraga is training him, he won't have trouble sleeping. He might fall out from exhaustion during training," Cahya countered his sister.

"No, Cahya, everyone needs to start settling for the night." Calida walked away.

Suvan was the first to stand up. Jai could tell he was powerful. He was a little taller than Arrow, who was already taller than him. Suvan had big honey eyes, and his warm tawny skin was smooth, his muscles firm, and his shoulders broad. His body was built more like a Landkeeper than a Fireheart. He stood up and headed to the sleeping room. The remaining Flamethrowers headed to the room and unrolled their blankets as he and Arrow had earlier.

It was extremely cramped and reminded him of how he lived with Arka. Jai carefully stepped between people, some laying down, some still unrolling blankets and talking. He saw Suvan wave at him, and he headed toward him.

"I know it's tight, but you can make a spot here. Arin is on the other side of you . . . she snores a little. Hope that doesn't keep you up," Suvan shrugged his powerful shoulders.

"It'll be fine, thanks," Jai said as he unrolled his blanket. He was not tired because he had a nap earlier at the hut. He looked around, and everyone else was either whispering to the person next to them or falling asleep. They all probably had a long day, and they just returned from an hour-long night hunt.

"Good night, Jai," Arin propped her head up to look at him before turning around to sleep.

He turned around to see her gazing softly at him. A part of him wanted to start a conversation since he wasn't tired. But Arin looked exhausted. He smiled as her eyes fluttered.

"See you in the morning." Moments later, she was fast asleep.

He stared at the ceiling of the cabin and reflected on his day. It had been a crazy day. Never in a million years did he expect such a chain of events. However, the Universe knows what everyone needs. It had been years since Jai was comfortable enough to let his thoughts linger on the Exalted Sky, the embodiment of faith for all those who believe. It was a refreshing change to see people acting as a true community. He didn't know anyone well, but he liked the bond of friendship that everyone had for one another. Arrow was close to Calida, Cahya had the twins, and Suvan seemed close with Dysis. Everyone mattered. Everyone had a place. They worked in unity for a common goal. Maybe there was more to Cyra than what she was given credit for. She was long gone, but her faithful followers remained. Despite whatever she did wrong, they believed in her so much as to accept him without question.

For the first time, Jai felt he had permission to set an expectation for his life and the power to define a legacy for himself. This would have never happened if he hadn't tried to restore life to Arrow. One person brought him face to face with a destiny he never could have imagined. The soft sound of Arin snoring was likened to an oddly comforting lullaby to Jai. He was amazed that all the Flamethrowers seemed immediately tired once they lay down, and most of them were fast asleep. Calida seemed to know best and presented herself as a fair and effective leader.

Jai lay awake feeling a subtle burning sensation within him. He quieted his mind, slowly visualizing the sensation.

In the darkness of the vast and endless sea, within every person lay a small flame. It burns with a determined and unwavering light, hungry for more fuel to sustain its existence. Without more fuel, the flame would die in the sea of darkness. The flame must search through that black canvas and overcome the obstacles and challenges that threaten to extinguish its fragile light. As it perseveres, it grows, driven by an innate desire to fulfill its potential. With each new obstacle, the flame burns brighter and hotter, fueled by the knowledge that its purpose is out there, waiting to be discovered. As it continues to burn, its purpose becomes clearer with each passing moment. Jai's flame knew that the journey was long and treacherous, but it was determined to find its place in the world and make a difference.

Like the flame in the sea of darkness, everyone must search for their purpose with a burning passion and an unyielding determination. They must navigate the challenges and obstacles that come their way, fueled by the knowledge that their purpose is out there, waiting to be discovered. For in the end, it is the flame that burns the brightest that will leave the greatest impact on the world.

Jai didn't think he was tired because he had slept earlier, but Arin's soft snoring eventually lulled him to sleep.

CHAPTER 5

J ai heard the thunder of footsteps all about him but wanted to rest a few moments longer. A clumsy kick to his side woke him up. He sat up clutching his ribs. He took a slow, deep breath to ease the pain.

"Look, you stepped on him! I told you to be careful," Arin hissed.

"I didn't mean to. I'm just big! I have big hands, arms, legs—and feet, not to mention it's cramped in here," Suvan whispered, "besides, your snoring probably kept him awake all night, so don't lecture me."

Jai sat up slowly and folded his legs. His vision was slightly hazy from sleep.

"Man, I didn't mean to kick you," Suvan stood looking down toward Jai.

"No problem. I was waking up anyway. Is everyone getting ready to go?"

"Yes, we are," Arin replied as Suvan walked to the socializing area. "I was going to wake you up with everyone else, but I felt bad that my snoring might have kept you up." Arin looked away, embarrassed.

Jai smiled as he stood up, "It didn't bother me at all, honestly. So what do we do now?"

"We are waiting for Cahya, Alena, and Arrow to come back, and then we'll leave for Pyroc. Calida already left this morning. We are going to meet her at the shortcut route."

"I'm going to wash up, okay?"

"That's fine. We aren't going to leave without you," Arin smiled before walking to join Suvan. Jai went into the washroom and washed his face with his hands. He rinsed his mouth and ran his fingers through his black hair, desperately attempting to neaten it from its usual mess of knots. When he came out of the washroom, Cahya, Alena, and Arrow had returned.

"Jai, are you ready to go? We should get there by early afternoon," Arrow called to him.

"Yeah, I'm ready," Jai replied. Everyone waved and wished them a successful trip. Jai sighed, trying to inhale the pleasant energy from the cabin.

"Hey, good luck with your training. Sheraga is one of the best people alive to teach you! I wish I was coming too," Suvan lightly punched Jai's arm. Arrow rolled his eyes in annoyance.

"I'll do my best and tell you about it when I return. Good luck with your post!"

Jai followed Arrow, Cahya, and the twins into the thick brush. The forest was mesmerizing during the early morning. The delicate shadows from the leaves danced on the lush forest floor. Jai wanted to laugh at himself for ever being nervous in the forest. He took a moment to notice that everyone had bows and arrows.

Why are they armed? Are they expecting to run into trouble?

Arrow and Cahya even had firebombs clipped on their belts. Jai pondered over this, especially since they were all gifted Firehearts. The Flamethrowers' movements were quick and deliberate.

"Cahya, take the lead," Arrow whispered. Cahya dashed to the front and looked up to see the sun shining through the leaves of the thick forest canopy. Jai looked around, but he didn't see the twins anymore. Before he could ask where they were, "They fell back. This is usually how we travel. In case an animal or person ambushes us, we have backup. Alena and Arin see us, but we can't see them. Don't worry," Arrow reassured Jai.

"Who would be trying to ambush you?"

Arrow scratched the back of his head, "Anyone associated with Agni."

Agni! That name again. "What does he want with the Flamethrowers?"

"We are the last remnants of Cyra's acolytes. Agni hates that we aren't buying into his regime."

"What is his regime?"

"Honestly, I don't know. All I can say is that Agni despises everything the past Legends did. Especially Cyra and Aenon."

"What did they do that, so many years later, Agni has a problem with it?"

Arrow sighed, "Long story short, they broke some Universal Laws and Cyra pretty much started the People's War."

"Damn!"

"Yeah, that's how most of us feel."

They traveled like this for several hours, with Cahya darting between trees with Arrow and Jai walking steadily behind him, the twin still unseen. Jai was tired from walking. He couldn't tell how long they had been traveling, and he was only growing more tired.

Cahya came to an abrupt stop and quickly used a wrist sling to shoot a short arrow into the top of a tall tree, "We're here," Cahya told Arrow. Alena and Arin dashed from the brush and joined them.

"Arrow, no one has followed us," Arin explained.

"That's very good," Calida whispered, walking from behind the tall trees. Only Jai seemed surprised by her presence. "The short route is clear for travel. This way, we don't have to go through Upper Ember. We should make it to Pyroc in a few hours," Calida explained.

A few hours?

Jai's legs trembled at the thought of more walking. It was evident that the Flamethrowers have more issues with Agni supporters than they initially let on. Between the feverish marking of trees and keeping half of their party covered at all times, they clearly had a history with Agni.

As Calida was talking, Cahya was making bird calls. A few minutes passed before a dark-brown messenger hawk perched itself onto Cahya's arm. Calida gave Arrow a folded message. He read it and handed it to Cahya. After Cahya had read the letter, he carefully rolled it into a tiny container. He attached it to the hawk's leg. The secrets that Calida, Arrow, and Cahya were holding were beginning to bother Jai as much as the thought of something he didn't know wanting him dead.

Once the hawk flew off, Calida took the lead, Arrow and Cahya ran into the brush, and the journey continued. Alena and Arin walked close to Jai as Calida darted forward. The silence was killing Jai.

I don't like this at all! What the hell have I gotten myself into? Either way I need to learn how to use some fire. Whether I leave or stay with the Flamethrowers, there's apparently a bounty over my head. If there are Firehearts after me, I won't survive with what I know how to do.

Jai could feel a gaze upon him. He turned, and Arin caught his attention; she raised her thin black eyebrows. "What are we going to do once we get there?" Jai whispered.

"Request an audience with the DragonLord," she whispered back.

"DragonLord sounds like a big deal. Is it a guarantee that he will train me?"

"Once he sees your eyes, he will. It's an honor to do a service for a Legend," Arin replied.

"How long is the training?"

"I don't know. I've never seen a Pyrocean training before. Alena and I are from Kindle, and training varies from region to region. I heard the Pyrocean training is rigorous, and I know Suvan trained in Pyroc."

"Even though he's an Emberite?"

"He's from Upper Ember. He did some military training with the DragonGuard. Suvan's family was very well off. They were not happy when he quit halfway through his program," Arin explained. "But he didn't train with the DragonLord, but under the mentorship of the DragonGuard."

I wonder why he quit.

"So why do I have to train with him?"

"The DragonLord has the spirit of the powerful dragon within him, which enhances all of his abilities. Your abilities are advanced but dormant from the lack of use. Only someone powerful can push you hard enough to see exactly what your abilities are, then teach you how to handle them."

"Oh, okay." This made Jai nervous; he had a hard time using fire in general. What was he going to do, blind the DragonLord?

"Jai, just relax and show him what you've got. You're going there to learn, not challenge him. Just focus on learning as best as you can," Alena whispered.

"You're right, I guess," Jai agreed. He gently nudged Arin, "How does the DragonLord have the spirit of a dragon?"

"I don't really know. Honestly, Pyroceans are very different from the rest of the Firehearts. They even go through physical changes as they use their element. But it all goes back to the presence of the dragon energy. That's all I know. You would have to ask Arrow for more information," Arin whispered.

"Physical changes?"

"Yeah, Pyroceans can have scales and some of their body parts can morph into dragon form."

Jai's mouth dropped. Then he remembered what Arrow said about common abilities in Pyroc seeming unusual to others.

"I heard that a long time ago, there was this sacred dragon that ruled Pyroc, and the first DragonLord killed that sacred dragon and ate its only egg. That's why Pyroceans have blood-colored hair as a symbol of the blood of the sacred dragon's only offspring," Alena added quietly.

Jai's eyes went wide. Arin rolled her eyes and shook her head, "That's only a rumor."

Alena laughed, clutching her stomach in amusement, "I made you scared! You should have seen the look on your face!"

"Alena, you're too loud," hissed Calida from ahead, "and you shouldn't be filling Jai's head with rumors. He has enough to focus on."

"Yes, Calida," Alena sighed.

Jai noticed that Alena was a little down after the reprimand. Arin nudged him, "She's fine, don't worry about it. After your first training day, Alena and I can show you our favorite place in Pyroc. It's a candy crystal shop. You'll love it," Arin smiled, showing her dimple.

"I've heard of candy crystals but never tried any."

"You have to try the flaming cherry," Arin squeaked.

"No, he has to try the hot chocolate," Alena smiled, wiggling her thin eyebrows.

"My favorite thing is the cozy atmosphere of the shop. The lady who owns it is so nice. It gives me fuzzy feelings just remembering it," said Arin, beaming with happiness.

"Almost there," Calida called quietly. Silence fell upon everyone. It may have been anticipation for the others, but it was nerves for Jai. He was excited and nervous at the same time. It was unbelievable to Jai that nearly an entire day had passed. Talking to Arin and Alena put him at ease about his expectation for training.

They were making their way through the dense forest, and Jai was preoccupied with navigating through the trees. However, he couldn't help but notice Arin's presence. Her hand would brush against his as they walked. Then their gaze would meet for mere moments before they both looked away. Jai couldn't help but feel a little flustered, but he wasn't sure if he was reading too much into things. In Lower Ember, his work kept him from mingling much with young people his age. Most of the girls got married off around sixteen, mostly for financial reasons. Jai rarely had the opportunity to talk to young women around his age. The Flamethrower ladies were all very beautiful, however there was something different about Arin. He simply enjoyed her conversation… and her presence.

From his peripheral vision, he could see Arrow and Cahya coming toward them. "So, we're basically here. Cahya, go ahead and send word to Dysis that we've arrived and relay that to Suvan," Arrow directed. Cahya nodded and began to make bird calls, summoning another messenger hawk. Calida and Arrow took the lead together. However, Arrow rolled his eyes repeatedly as he huffed.

Jai looked on with wonder at the volcano ahead of them. Its heat was mesmerizing. He sighed. Never had he felt so warm before. He felt his energy renewed.

This feels like paradise.

His muscles instantly relaxed as if he had been wrapped in a blanket. His breath was even, his nerves had quieted. He was in a state of complete peace and felt renewed.

"That's why Calida told us to go to sleep. The heat from the volcano makes it hard to sleep out here," Alena explained. Jai could feel the rejuvenating effects of the volcano. How could anyone hate this place? The landscape was a chain of volcanoes, some active to the far west and the dormant ones to the east. There were far more dormant volcanoes than active ones. Civilization had settled at the volcano bases. The grass and trees were surprisingly lush compared to the surrounding volcanoes. There were many beautifully crafted stone houses. Some houses were made of beige stone, and others were light gray. There was nothing dreary in sight.

Off to the west was a large home—more like a palace. It was made of beige stone and trimmed in carefully crafted gold. The doors were also gold, and soldiers with spears decked in wine-colored uniforms were visible as well. The roof was the color of terracotta. The palace was a beautiful sight. Jai leaned close to Arin, pointing to it, "Who lives there?"

"The DragonLord's family," she whispered as her breath tickled his ears.

"Calida, are we going through the city?" Alena asked.

"No, we are going to travel along the outskirts until we reach the palace," Calida asserted.

Cahya was running behind them, "I sent the message and received one as well." He passed it to Arrow. Once Arrow finished reading it, he gave it to Calida. She took her time with the message before exhaling heavily.

"Stay together. We're almost there," Calida commanded. They walked for about thirty minutes at a brisk pace. When they were almost half a mile from the palace, Calida gave Arrow a black hood.

He refused to accept it and pushed her hand away. "I'm not going to hide from anyone," he spat, rolling his eyes.

"I just thought it would help," Calida raised her voice, clearly irritated with how Arrow responded.

"I know, I'm sorry," he replied gently. Calida looked at him with gentle eyes and carefully grabbed his left hand with her right one. She didn't let go until they reached the palace. Several feet from the door, the guards simultaneously formed a line keeping them from entering.

"State your business!" one male guard commanded. Jai observed them. There were men and women soldiers, all in wine uniforms. The only distinguishing difference was that the golden breastplates were shaped differently for the male and female bodies. An opening toward the back of their gold helmets allowed their blood-red colored ponytails to be pulled through. All the ponytails were different lengths but never changed in color.

Arrow took a step toward the guard, "Urgent business for the DragonLord about the Soul of the Sun."

The guard raised his thick blood-red eyebrow. The faint jade color scales near his eyes seemed to grow darker with his irritation, "Asahi?"

"It's Arrow," he growled in reply, tenting his thinner, longer red brows.

The guard hissed, "You shouldn't even be here." The man hissed and stepped forward, bringing himself eye to eye with Arrow. The faint scales began to glow, and an unsettling energy plagued the air. The rest of the warriors seemed to also have scales on their faces. The scales were glowing bright jade.

Arrow brought his face closer to the guard's. "I dare you to raise a hand at me."

"With pleasure!"

Calida and Cahya bristled and raised their bows, but they were quickly surrounded by the Pyrocean soldiers, pointing red-tipped lances at them.

"Call them back," Arrow growled.

"Spoiled prince, why don't you make me? Oh, you can't, exiled prince. Seems like you forgot that you don't have any status or authority anymore."

"I'll show you authority!"

Calida's eyes widened, "Arrow, we need to de-escalate!"

"Come on, Asahi! I'm waiting—we all know you're no dragon," the guard taunted.

A wild orange fire with hints of green and blue covered Arrow's hands as he stepped toward the guard. The soldiers only continued pressing their lances deathly close.

"Enough! Pyre, call the soldiers back," shouted a tall, broad-shouldered man with a bright cluster of jade scales outlining his intense amber eyes. His waist-length blood-red hair flowed behind him as he descended the stairs.

"Dragons, ease!" Pyre called. Instantly, they all reformed the line around the palace. The odd energy immediately ceased. The man with the long hair slowly walked down the stone steps of the palace toward them. His skin was a rich shade of brown with copper undertones, enhancing the intensity of his eyes. He wore a long, wine-colored robe that looked like it was made of satin with a golden dragon covering most of the front. He had black pants and boots with gold tips. When he reached the bottom of the steps, he said, "Asahi, choose two of your guests to accompany you inside."

Jai and the Flamethrowers appeared uneasy about separating, especially after what just transpired.

"Calida, I can stay out here with Alena and Arin." Cahya suggested.

"That's fine with me," Calida replied.

"I am not Asahi! I am Arrow!" he hissed. "Calida, Jai, come with me." Pyre allowed the three of them through. Jai caught Arin's gaze as she mouthed the words, "be careful." He heeded her warning as the trio followed the man back into the palace.

CHAPTER 6

S tepping through the grand entrance of the palace, they were immediately engulfed in a regal atmosphere exuding power and prestige. The air was thick with the aroma of freshly cut flowers and a hint of incense. The high ceilings were adorned with intricate gold-painted carvings. A row of towering gold columns lined the grand hall, creating a sense of opulence and grandeur. Each column was ornately decorated with intricate patterns of blooming flowers, shimmering with the glint of gold leaf. Walking along the gleaming floor of polished marble, Jai couldn't help but feel small in the presence of such magnificence.

Wine-red rugs led the way to the thrones of the DragonLord and DragonLady, positioned at the end of the hall. The rich hue of the rugs perfectly complemented the grandeur of the gold columns and trim. The thrones themselves were works of art. The DragonLord's throne was adorned with a towering golden dragon with outstretched wings that seemed to take flight. The DragonLady's throne was equally grand with a delicate golden dragon weaving its way around the armrests. The thrones were as comfortable as they were grand, with plush cushions and richly embroidered silk upholstery. Dragon lanterns with intricate patterns cast a warm glow over the hall, and their light flickered softly against the gilded walls. The palace created a sense of awe-inspiring beauty.

The DragonLady's chair was occupied by a slender woman in a red floor-length dress with capped sleeves. She wore what looked like a gold and diamond choker, matching the rings that adorned both of her hands. Her long, blood-red hair was pulled back into one long braid with the end laid in her lap. The woman was beautiful with her soft amber eyes and golden brown skin. She looked like a queen. The man headed toward the empty seat to the right of her. Arrow stopped halfway to their throne, causing Calida and Jai to follow suit.

Once the man took his seat, he asked Arrow, "Whatever are you doing here, brother?"

Arrow was fuming angrily, "I'm doing you a favor." Calida gently touched his shoulder, calming him slightly.

Arrow's brother looked slightly annoyed, "I only asked you a question. No need to get aggressive and hostile, especially in the presence of my queen, Liora. You're in my house, and I've never wronged you, so drop that crap at the door. I can clearly see that your guest is the famed Soul of the Sun—or a Legend, as they are now called. Is this the favor that you claim to be bringing me? Don't answer that. Bringing him to me means that he needs help with his gift, which is work for me. Get your head on straight and talk with some sense."

The energy in the room became hostile. The area around Sheraga's eyes started to glow along with the jade dragon scales. The glare in his eyes became deadly. He never looked away from Arrow. He leaned forward ever so slightly. His front teeth transformed into long, glistening white fangs. His fingernails curled into black claws. Jai was frozen with pure shock. He could hear Calida gulp loudly;

her nerves were just as frazzled as his. Sheraga's queen just looked at his beastly transformation with pride twinkling in her eyes.

"Do it! Come on! Isn't this the moment you've been waiting for, brother? Isn't this the kind of DragonLord you want to be? Known for war and bloodshed."

"If you know me so well, you'd be wise not to tempt my hand."

"Arrow . . ." Calida whispered.

"Like I said, come and get me!"

Jai turned to Arrow, "What are you—"

Arrow disappeared from his sight. Sheraga lunged at the Flamethrower with the speed of a raging beast, slamming Arrow into the wall of the palace with a violent thud!

Sheraga laughed, "Finally trying to be a man? It's about time. Mother would have loved to have seen this, wouldn't she?"

"Let me go!"

"Make me!"

Calida grabbed her bow. As she reached back to her quiver for an arrow, Liora leaped forward with a golden lance, blocking Calida's hand. Liora's eyes suddenly manifested bright purple scales underneath as she pressed the blade of her lance against Calida's neck. "Don't move. I don't want to hurt you. But if I have to, I will."

Calida held her breath as her life teetered in Liora's hands.

Jai yelled, "Can we just talk about this?"

Arrow growled at Sheraga, "Let her go!" He squirmed against Sheraga's body weight, unable to free himself.

"I thought you were a man! What's wrong? You did ask for this. Where's all that attitude? 'Come and get me,' did I hear that right? Well, I've got you now."

There was something in the way Sheraga was talking that convinced Jai that Sheraga was enjoying this. He had to do something. Lifting his hand, light beamed directly into Liora's eyes. She dropped her lance and covered her eyes, groaning.

Calida fell to her knees, trembling and gasping for air.

Sheraga's attention was immediately on Liora. "Li!"

He effortlessly threw Arrow into the palace column, and the impact ricocheted through the hall. Arrow's body fell limp upon impact.

Suddenly, Jai found his neck gripped by Sheraga's claws. "Li, are you all right?"

Liora brushed off her shoulders before placing her foot on the back of Calida's neck. "I'm fine, he just blinded me."

Jai could feel his veins pulsating, but he felt no fear.

"How dare you walk through these doors and assault my wife, the DragonLady of Pyroc!"

"And you?" Jai huffed.

"What?" Sheraga's amber eyes narrowed.

"You're looking me dead in the eyes. I'm clearly a Legend and you're ready to rip my throat out. Go ahead, kill me. Dying would be a luxury right about now."

"Jai, no," Calida's eyes pleaded.

"Enough! Let them go, Sheraga. They aren't the problem," Arrow staggered to his feet. "You win, Sheraga! As always, you're always right. You always win. It's always you."

Arrow stood and hung his head, "Train him Sheraga. That's why we're here, why I'm here. Do your esteemed duty. He has a unique gift but needs help to master the flame. Train him. I'll leave. I know I'm not welcome here. Just promise to train him, and I will return to my exile. I swear on our mother's grave that I will never step foot here ever again. Forgive me . . . for everything," Arrow turned to leave.

Sheraga's eyes softened. His claws withdrew to normal fingernails; his fangs shrunk. He loosened his grip on Jai. Looking to Liora, whose purple scales were fading away, "Let the girl go."

Liora lifted her foot, and Calida gasped for air. Arrow was clutching his arm as he slowly walked toward the palace entrance.

"Arrow," Calida and Jai called to him simultaneously.

The Pyrocean ignored them.

"Brother, you know you can't escape him," Sheraga called out.

"He doesn't care, so neither do I."

A flash of blue and green flames overtook the entrance.

"Whoever allowed you in this palace?" came a roar at the entrance. Arrow jumped backward, to keep from being burned. Jai began to sweat profusely. It was like he was being baked in an oven. He looked over to Calida, her clothes were soaked.

"Father, I had it under control," Sheraga started. He walked briskly to the entrance and stood between Arrow and the roaring fire. Jai looked around but he did not see anyone.

"No! Asahi made his own choices and is still banished from these lands," their father roared but never showed himself.

"All right, I'm leaving now!" Arrow shouted as he gathered himself. Fire spewed feverishly from the door. Arrow quickly jumped back; Sheraga never moved.

"You are allowed to leave when I allow you to leave," an older man in gold robes appeared, strong and powerful. His red hair fell past his shoulders; it was not as silky as Sheraga's, probably becoming lackluster with age. He had Arrow's complexion but Sheraga's eyes, build, and broad nose. "How dare you show up here and disrespect your brother, the DragonLord, with your tone? I banished you! You are an exile, stripped of your title! You left your brother during a military engagement and then ran away from home. Your absence grieved your ill mother to death. We begged you to come and pay your respects, and you never came to her burial. Then you missed your brother's wedding and coronation and showed up a year later asking for favors!"

"Why do you keep bringing that up? That's not all that I am. Look, I brought the Legend!"

Sheraga stood between Arrow and their father, "Brother, stop!"

"You may have brought the Soul of the Sun, but he needs to hear what type of man you really are. Maybe he'll find that you're no man." Their father pushed Sheraga aside with ease. He shook Arrow angrily, "You're no dragon! Look at you! You're no dragon at all."

Sheraga looked down, a deep sorrow in his eyes. "Father of Dragons, I'll handle Asahi with a firm hand," Sheraga calmly stated. Bhasker nodded to his son and left, using a flame and walking into a spewing blue fire, just like he entered.

"You're not going to put a hand on him, not with me standing here!" Calida yelled at Sheraga. Liora snatched Calida backward by her ponytail. The Flamethrower leader turned with her fist raised. Liora caught her hand with ease.

"Look, woman, don't address me like that. Liora, ease. Leave us to discuss our business without distraction," Sheraga looked at the beautiful Pyrocean woman.

"Of course, my love," Liora replied, releasing Calida's hand. The ladies walked outside. Liora brushed her fingertips across Sheraga's back as she and Calida made their exit.

Sheraga sighed deeply as he walked back toward his throne, "I was trying to avoid that, brother. I hope you know that."

"Avoid it? You attacked me! And Jai, the freaking Legend! You weren't trying to avoid anything!"

Jai huffed, "Arrow, relax. You can't blame Sheraga for everything. You weren't being respectful of his position from the start," Jai contended.

"Now you're blaming me! We're here because of—"

"I'm not blaming you. But if I'm your problem, I will leave. I have no problems with handling myself. I don't need you to take care of me. You were dead a couple of days ago, and I saved you. I had to run for my life because I helped you."

"Dead?" Sheraga questioned.

Arrow was furious, "Is that how—"

"Brother, shut up! I'm sick of this! I'm sick of your immaturity! I don't know what version of events you're telling, but no one has done anything to you. You've grown up with the best of everything. You've been a pampered second son, wandering around without a purpose! I've done nothing but support you. I practically raised you, you ungrateful, unbearable brat!"

Arrow trembled, "I'm—"

"Shut up! You know your problem? You want what I have without doing the work. Now you've gotten in such a bad row with Father. It's shameful how you treat him. It's shameful how you've treated us."

"I know, I know," Arrow started pacing, "I didn't mean for any of this to happen! I am sorry for the disgrace I've brought this family. I'm ready for your firm hand."

Sheraga chuckled, "Firm hand? I've already roughed you up. Arrow, you've always made your own trouble. You're so rebellious. You must always be right, even when you're not making sense. You always have to learn lessons the hard way. But, regardless, we are still brothers. I will always love you, even if you never love me."

"Sheraga—"

"I don't want to hear it. Here's my ultimatum. I'll train Jai after you initiate a heart-to-heart talk with Father. I want you to be here to experience certain aspects of training with him since you are traveling together. And you can't stay here without Father's approval. If I could repeal your exile, I would, but we both know I can't do that."

"Or I can take him somewhere else," Arrow growled.

Sheraga laughed at Arrow's remark. "Who? Your only options are me, Father, or Tora. I'm giving you an ultimatum. Father won't do it, and Tora has other major things on his hands," Sheraga reminded.

"No, I want you to train me! Everyone is telling me that you're the best, and that's what I need. Arrow, you have to make things right with your family . . . and be thankful that you have one. Where I'm from, having a family is a luxury . . . one most of us can't afford," Jai looked Arrow in the eye, serious about wanting Sheraga's training.

"Come on, Sheraga, who's the DragonLord here?" Arrow huffed, rolling his eyes.

"I am the DragonLord. I don't hold the Dragon Spirit yet. Father will pass the Spirit to me once I'm ready. What matters is that I have gone through coronation and am the official DragonLord."

"You really believe that?" Arrow rolled his eyes as he sat down on the floor a few feet from Sheraga. Jai continued to stand, watching the interaction between the brothers.

"Of course, he has no reason to teach me all of this to be lying to me. The Dragon Spirit will fuse with me once it feels I am ready for it. Father is actually unable to keep the Dragon Spirit once it is ready to bond with me. Just like every other DragonLord before me. Besides, I know that I have to work on my thirst for battle before I'm ready to hold the Dragon Spirit; otherwise, I will just throw Pyroc into war after war," Sheraga admitted.

"Arrow, you have to make up with Father. I'm serious. Don't let the same thing that happened with Mother happen with Father. You and I both know that's why you didn't come to the burial. You couldn't admit that you were wrong."

"You're not mad that I missed your wedding and coronation?" Arrow asked with his head down.

"Of course I was upset. We're brothers . . . I thought we were closer than that. But I wanted that day to be perfect for Liora. She deserved that. I wanted my father to be happy. He deserved that. I wanted a wedding that our mother would have been proud of. Her memory deserved that. You're my brother. Pyrocean blood is—"

"Forged by the heart of dragons," Arrow finished the statement.

"Exactly, so by nature, we aren't weak. Weakness is against our nature. So, be a man, be a dragon, and go to Father. And Arrow, if you get scared, just remember that he loves you." Sheraga and Arrow stood and embraced each other, and Sheraga patted Arrow's back.

"Jai, stay here with my brother until I come back." Arrow left the palace by fire as his father did before him.

Jai sighed heavily.

"Forgive me for handling you. Since the founding of Pyroc, we have always closely aligned and supported the Fireheart Legend, or Soul of the Sun as we prefer to call your kind. Honestly, it was more of a reaction. I thought you attacked Liora."

"I understand. I was in a tough position. I didn't want anyone to get hurt. I only blinded her so she would let Calida go, hoping that Arrow would calm down. Calida means as much to Arrow as your wife means to you."

"I see. I hope I didn't give you a bad impression," Sheraga chuckled.

"No, the opposite. You seem like a good leader. Protecting your wife was a natural reaction, and I expected you to respond with force. I may not be able to utilize fire, but I'm not weak."

"Duly noted."

"That was a smart move having your brother make amends with your father. I would have wanted the same thing. I don't remember my family, and I don't like seeing others take their family for granted."

"Understood. What's wrong with your gift?"

"I don't know. I can use light, and the light can heal, but I have a hard time turning light into fire. Sometimes it works, other times it doesn't," Jai explained.

"Light and healing, huh? That's a new one. The rest is easy to fix," Sheraga plainly stated.

"Really? That makes me feel pretty stupid," Jai sighed.

"Don't feel that way. A lot of Firehearts have that problem. It's common, so you shouldn't feel bad about that. You just need time and space, and you'll have it down quickly."

"I hope I'm not prying but it seems like Arrow has a rift—"

Sheraga laughed, "Seems like! I don't know where all that is coming from. However, I suppose it's my fault. Our mother had horrific childbirths. Pyroceans are a bit different. A baby is born, and then our mothers birth our dragon energy. I had a very powerful dragon energy that created a difficult birthing experience for my mother. After me, my parents didn't think they would have any more children. My rigorous training to prepare me for the throne started at five. I was eight when my brother was born; he was breech, and the birth nearly killed my mother. She spent the rest of her life on bed rest."

"In a normal royal family, the royal-born DragonLord or Lady is the sole one preparing the heir to rule. The other parent, be it the father or mother, raises the other children. In our case, our mother could not raise Arrow. So I did. Father had little time. He was consumed with preparing me to rule and searching the world for the best doctors to try and heal my mother. I took my little brother nearly everywhere, and I tried to teach him everything I knew."

"I don't understand why he treats you like this!"

"See these scales? See how vibrant they are?"

Jai nodded.

"It's pure dragon energy. Once boys go through puberty, we get these scales under our eyes. But girls' scales are very faint. They grow prominent if they are upset or angry, and they appear in the most beautiful colors. They're purple or pink, or even a soft mint. Absolutely beautiful! Due to our mother's sickness, Arrow's dragon energy is a little . . . severed. He can't keep the scales on his face. So you know how we men can be. No one messed with him while I was around, but I could not be there all the time. That was the beginning of him not seeing me as a brother but as a rival."

"In a way I get it. I'm a Legend and I can't use fire. It's uncomfortable at times. But it doesn't make me less of a man. Arrow has a lot going for him. Seems like he grew up trying to be you and has become hateful because that's not possible."

"I tried everything I could. I'd rather us just fight it out, but my father would not approve of that. I already know I'm going to get an earful for roughing him up earlier."

"You could have killed him."

"Ha! That! I could have, but I pride myself on exercising restraint."

Jai furrowed his brows. It was apparent that he and Sheraga had different ideas of restraint.

CHAPTER 7

As the crackling sound of the roaring flames filled the air, Arrow took a deep breath and steeled himself for what lay ahead. He knew that he had disappointed his father in a way that would take more than mere words to make amends. So, with his resolve firm and his heart heavy, he accepted the flames of the raging inferno. The heat was intense, scorching the air and making it difficult to breathe. Arrow had not flame traveled in a long time. This sensation felt nearly foreign to him. How long has it been since he'd left? He felt his dragon energy rumble, a sensation that had been dormant for far too long. His eyes itched; he could feel the imprint of scales burning its way close to his eyes. The tongues of flame licked at his clothes, threatening to singe his skin, but Arrow's dragon energy did not fail him.

He felt like he had been in the flame for hours, although he knew it was only minutes. He didn't want to admit how much he missed this sensation. Finally, after so many years, he felt connected to his roots and family legacy. A surging power called to his soul. The essence of everything he was wanted to grab and consume the wild energy. But he knew that he was unworthy. Sheraga's words echoed in his mind. Weakness is against our nature.

However, he always felt that he was the weak link in the family. The ancient dragons would have been disgusted by him. That essential piece of who he was, son of the DragonLord, second-born Dragon Prince, and brother of the Crown Prince, was missing. He couldn't find it in him to embrace the fire. As quickly as the surge came, it left him. He could feel the presence of his father. Flame traveling, the ability to move from one area of fire to another, was a gift that only the family of the DragonLords possessed.

His father was standing at the top of a dormant volcano, gazing into his eyes. The guilt of unworthiness humbled him, "Father . . . I knew I was wrong to leave

Sheraga in the middle of a military exercise like that. He could have gotten killed because of me. The commotion disrupted the men on the border of Lower Ember, and it escalated. It was my fault, and I ran when the first person was killed. I know I looked like a coward in front of the entire DragonGuard. I just wanted to prove that I was as strong as Sheraga. When I came home, I heard you and mother talking about what positions would be passed to us. DragonLord for Sheraga and the two of you wanted to send me to school. I was a failure—like I should have never been born to you."

"My stubborn son, but my son nonetheless." The raging anger in his father's eyes slowly dissipated, and a warm expression replaced the fury. "Asahi, we just wanted to buy you some time. You weren't ready to take an official title, but Sheraga was ready. We couldn't hold him back. He was taking his duties seriously, and he focused on his goals and his passions. He chose a suitable wife and was ready for life as the future DragonLord. You let other people distract you from your most important duty."

"You don't understand what it's like!"

"Then tell me!"

"You have no idea what it's like to be in his shadow! Sheraga! Sheraga! Sheraga! He's so strong! He's so brave! He's the future! I couldn't compete with him! He has an eight-year advantage over me. You don't have siblings. You don't get it."

"Compete? Asahi, son, this is a family, not a competition. If Sheraga had been born blind and void of all his limbs, he would still be next in line to be DragonLord."

"I know." Arrow's shoulders went limp as he hung his head.

"Asahi, you've been so distracted from your most important duty."

"The legacy of the dragons?"

"No!" His father grabbed his shoulders and slightly shook him, "Finding the dragon in you! That is your duty. You are a son of the DragonLord family, and power and strength come from this alone. It's an essence that calls you, then you claim it, become one with it."

Arrow hugged Bhasker, "Father, forgive me. I just wanted to be Sheraga. I wanted to be needed. I just want to be great like you and him. Every time I look within, I don't see anyone worthy. I'm not half as strong as Sheraga and hardly as wise as you."

Bhasker let Arrow go and smiled, "I paid a mighty price for what I know today. Sheraga paid the price to be as strong as he is today.

"My mother was the DragonLady, and she lived after the time of Cyra of Kindle. My mother loved to go on adventures and travel. She was older when she married and gave birth to me. We lost my father to war when I was sixteen. After my father's death, she passed the Dragon Spirit on to me."

"At sixteen?"

"Yes. She moved to a dormant volcano and told me I could visit her three times a year, never any more. She also told me that whenever I was going through something good or bad to ask myself, 'what is the Universe trying to teach me?' That was the greatest thing she could have done for me. I learned to appreciate her time and wisdom by giving me only three chances to visit. By turning to the Universe, I learned something from everything I went through. My father taught me how to fight, lead, be a man, and accept responsibility. My mother taught me how to listen to the lessons of the Universe.

"The price was paid through mistakes. I made many, but I never repeated them. Sheraga paid the price to be strong. He spent countless hours training and learning war, strategy, and tactics. He devoted himself to the soldiers and taught them what he learned, creating unity among them. He paid with his time. The best of who we are always comes with the price we must pay to acquire it."

"What am I?"

"You have to tell me. You have to find the dragon in you and own the unique energy that comes with it. Everyone is different. Son, once you find it, never let it go! Once you own it, it in turn will guide you to become everything you were meant to be. Son, I never hated you. I was more hurt than angry. Think about your mother; she grew ill and she just wanted to live long enough to see you both grow to be something great. It killed me that I could not make that wish come true for her. It tore my soul to watch my beloved son toss away his birthright and glory. Your future will always be a part of my legacy, and I love you. Come home, son. I want to reinstate you and end your exile, but you must give me an explanation for a few things. Why did you leave your brother during the soldier's exercise?"

"Fear. I was afraid of my mistakes. I knew I wasn't powerful enough to stop or fix them. I was afraid of showing the soldiers that they were right about me not being as strong as Sheraga," Arrow admitted.

"Why did you run away?"

"I felt unworthy of being your son. You and Mother planned to announce Sheraga as the next DragonLord, and it felt like I failed because both of you knew there was no palace position for me to take."

"Why didn't you come to your mother's burial?"

"Guilt. I knew I was wrong in how I left. I felt guilty that I wasn't there for her like she was there for me. She was always there for me."

"Why didn't you come to your brother's wedding and coronation?"

"Jealousy. I was jealous that he always had success and progress. I forgot that he was my brother and that he loved me. I forgot that I could hurt him. And when I remembered, I didn't care. Sheraga always looked after me. He never boasted. He was always proud to call me his brother. I was jealous when I called him my brother."

"So from now on, you must fight to never let fear, guilt, and jealousy rob you of important things in life—of your destiny. One day, I will expire; never let anyone divide you. The most important title you have is Brother. Live and learn. So here, I forgive, and we both put the past behind us, son," Bhasker held out his hand, and Arrow shook it. His father ended his exile.

"I wish Mother could have seen my growth, to see me trying now," Arrow whispered.

"We believe in the Universe. When good people die, their soul ascends to the Stars. It is those Stars that light our path. She knows what you have become. Son, no one wants to be wrong. But Kirana was always completely honest and accepted responsibility for her actions. And like you, her honesty brought good things her way. You brought the Soul of the Sun. You're making your legacy now.

"She worried about you a lot—worried that we were not giving you what you needed. But look, with a little effort from everyone, love, and forgiveness, we're doing grand things now. When the story gets told hundreds of years in the future, this Soul of the Sun's journey will start with you," Bhasker touched Arrow's shoulder. His father roared until fire erupted from his mouth. Something was comforting in the fury of flames as they stepped into the fire together. They moved back to the palace entrance from the dormant volcano, where Sheraga and Jai were waiting.

"From the looks on your faces, everything must have been positive. I formally accept the opportunity to train Jai the Legend. We begin in the morning. And Arrow, nice hair," Sheraga chuckled.

Jai watched Arrow pull the ends of his hair that fell toward his shirt collar; his hair was completely blood red.

"I don't know what happened!" Arrow gasped.

"You've healed the dragon within you," Bhaskar plainly stated.

Arrow smiled, then sighed in relief.

Noticing the faint outline of jade scales near Arrow's eyes, Jai was confused. He thought the Dragon Spirit was in Bhasker, and he had to give it to Sheraga. His thoughts were interrupted when Sheraga spoke to him, "You can stay in the palace while you're here. We will start tomorrow; however, I expect an important guest tomorrow, late morning, early afternoon."

"Thank you. I'm ready to try my best," Jai replied.

Liora entered with Calida, who ran toward Arrow. He

lovingly accepted her embrace, gently placing his chin on her head.

"Is everything okay? Is the mission secure? Did somebody beat you up?"

Arrow chuckled and playfully pulled away from her, "Yes, yes, and no."

Calida started squealing, "I knew you could do this!" She stood on her tiptoes to get as close to eye level as possible with him, "I'm so proud of you," she whispered.

Jai unintentionally cleared his throat. This caused Arrow and Calida to step away from each other, faces burning with embarrassment.

"How did things go with the DragonLady?"

"It was nice, you know we just talked... she's actually quite nice. Y-Your hair looks good, this is a different look for you," she replied nervously while twirling her hair between her fingers.

"Yeah, thanks. I think we should let the twins and your brother know we're good to go, right?"

"Yeah, I'll tell them." Calida left the palace. Liora walked past Arrow with pursed lips and giggled before taking her seat next to Sheraga.

"Brother, you can share your old room with Jai and the girl's brother," Sheraga said.

"Calida," Liora and Arrow said at the time.

"Calida's brother," Sheraga corrected.

"I'll prepare a room for the ladies," Liora said to Sheraga, who nodded.

"Thank you. Let's head upstairs, Jai," Arrow instructed. Jai followed Arrow up the stone stairs and into a large room, "Stay here while I grab some extra beds from another room."

"Okay. It's not like I'm going anywhere," Jai replied.

Arrow left, and Jai looked around at the enormous room. It was the size of the entire cabin back in the forest. The walls were ivory stone, and there was a large bed, three times the size of his old bed in Lower Ember. There were two mahogany wood chests in the room and a rectangular mirror over one of the chests. Arrow returned, pushing one bed before him and pulling another behind him.

"I could have helped you out. I'm not a child," Jai frowned and grabbed the bed in front of Arrow.

"I know, but I don't know what Sheraga has planned for you tomorrow. He has a reputation for training until you drop, and I know that from personal experience,"

Arrow replied. They set up the other two beds in different corners of the room to give everyone their private space.

Cahya ran up. "Man, look at all this. I still can't believe this is your place!"

"It's my brother's house, Cahya," Arrow rolled his eyes.

"Whatever. I'm going to enjoy it while it lasts," Cahya grinned and hopped belly-first onto the bed in the farthest corner. "I'm sleeping."

"Did you send all the messages?" Arrow asked while slowly laying down on his bed.

"Of course, I'm Cahya. I don't forget things like that," Cahya smirked. "Hey Jai, what's on your mind? You don't talk much."

"I have a lot on my mind. I wish I could remember my past and what happened the day Arka found me. I want to know why Zay and Arka wanted to kill me. I want to know who is this Agni that Zay works for and what he knows about me. I want to prove to myself that I can be what the Firehearts need me to be," Jai explained.

"Did you say, Agni?" Cahya asked.

"Yeah."

"What about Agni?" Cahya sat up, alert and ready to hear what Jai would say next.

"All he said was that he would have to tell Agni that I got away from him," Jai tried recalling what Zay said.

"Suvan said something about Agni about a month ago on one of his missions. Something about Upper Ember wanted to trade some glass products with Kindle, but Agni wouldn't allow it," Cahya reflected.

"Seems like the big question is what does Agni want with Jai and how does he know about him," Arrow said quietly as he looked up at the ceiling.

"Well, enough about that for now. What was your life like in Ember? What did you do for a living? Do you have any friends?" Cahya asked question after question.

"It was okay, I guess. Lower Ember is all that I've known. The day Arka found me, he asked what I was doing about town with no parents. I thought I was waiting for them. So he stayed with me until nightfall, but no one came to get me. So, he brought me home with him. I was scared of him at first. He liked to yell a lot. Then I realized that he was always loud like that. He gave me a home, and I never went hungry. Arka was a pretty good cook, which surprised me," Jai laughed a little bit.

"I grew to trust him. When I was twelve, he put me to work. He said I had to learn to do something with my hands if I was going to make it. He started bringing me to the workshop where he made weapons and sold them. I liked being by the fire, so he taught me how to use the cross peen. I had it much better than most people my age in Lower Ember. Zay—"

"The guy who killed me," Arrow interjected.

"He actually killed you?" Cahya asked.

"Yep, Jai brought me back," Arrow nodded.

"From the dead? No!"

Jai cleared his throat, "Zay, as I was saying, he had it hard. He lived in a tiny house in a remote town with his mother, who was blind from an eye injury. Zay was very young, but he worked hard. He walked miles daily, going from town to town to help his mother. She passed away when he was fourteen. He would hunt and sell his game for money, but it usually wasn't enough to get by. He was always looking for odd jobs so he wouldn't lose his mother's house. Life made him angry and unforgiving, but he has a lot of good."

"He killed me, so I'm not inclined to believe that," Arrow huffed.

"I'm not saying he hasn't done horrible things. I just hope things turn around for him because he has some good in him too." Jai shrugged his shoulders.

"He probably flipped out once he lost his mom," Cahya sighed. "Moms bring balance, and life is incredibly different when you don't have them there anymore."

"You lost your mom too?" Jai asked.

"No, she's alive. We just haven't seen her in a long time. She's been on an undercover mission for Upper Ember, investigating Agni. He's been trying to take charge by force. She would usually write to us, but she hasn't in a while," Cahya explained.

"What are we going to do for the rest of the day? I'm getting tired of resting at strange times! I have all this energy and want to do something," Jai grumbled, getting restless.

"You want to get a pet Komodo dragon?" Cahya asked, beaming with excitement.

"A pet what?"

"We are not doing that," Arrow raised his voice.

"Excuse me, what the Legend says goes, Crown Prince," Cahya teased.

"How often do I tell you not to call me that? I was never the Crown Prince. I'm the Dragon Prince!"

Cahya shrugged, "Same thing to me."

"What other things are there to do?" Jai asked, sensing Cahya was getting on Arrow's nerves.

"Anything a Fireheart could possibly think of! Obstacle courses over a flaming lake, the peppercorn challenge, eating spicy candy crystals, sightseeing, there's plenty to do," Cahya walked around the room frantically. "How old are you, Jai?"

"I'm nineteen," he was puzzled as to why Cahya randomly asked.

"I'm seventeen!"

"Oh, okay."

"Did you decide on what you want to do?"

Hmm, Cahya is not normally this wound up. This must be from the volcano. Even I feel a bit off.

"Arin and Alena wanted to get candy crystals. I guess we can do that," Jai stated.

"We can go tomorrow. Sheraga would kill me if I took you somewhere the day before you had training with him," Arrow raised his red eyebrows.

"What's training with him like?" Jai asked.

"It depends on what he's planning to teach you. Knowing him, he's probably in the war room with Liora discussing his ideas for training you—like the good old days. If he's in a talking mood, he'll give you more information with some demonstrations. If he's in a testing mood, you wanna get your sleep now. He won't stop until one of you drops . . . literally," Arrow advised.

"Well, maybe he'll be in a talking mood. He said that he had a guest coming tomorrow," Jai reflected.

"For your sake, I hope so," Cahya blinked. "Now Arrow, what's to eat?"

"Don't know. I can ask Baara, though. She does most of the cooking around here. Wait here, I'll be right back." Arrow got out of his bed and left.

"Hmmm, I wonder who Baara is. I'll be back," Cahya wiggled his eyebrows. He left with a mysterious twinkle in his eyes.

Jai opened his hands and allowed the light to flow. He focused and tried to turn the light into fire. No fire came. Jai thought that the intense heat from the volcano would enhance his ability, but that was not the case.

"Ugh, this is so annoying. Sometimes it works, sometimes it doesn't," Jai grumbled.

After about twenty minutes, Arrow and Cahya could be heard in the hall on the way to the room. "I really can't believe you. I said that I was coming back!" Arrow was clearly irritated with Cahya.

"I just wanted to know who Baara was, that's all, man," Cahya put his hands up and walked past Arrow and toward his corner. "She was beautiful, though," Cahya beamed, "so Jai, we are having spicy fish rolls and stir fry for dinner."

"Never had any of that before."

"Well, thanks to Cahya, Baara will be bringing the food in a little while," Arrow rolled his eyes.

"See, I got the food coming express! It's all thanks to my charm," Cahya boasted.

After another twenty minutes, a beautiful girl with pale amber eyes and tawny skin walked in with a large golden food tray. Her facial expression was angelic and innocent. There were pale violet scales outlining her eyes, giving her a near-ethereal appearance. "Dinner is ready," she said. Her voice was gentle, like her eyes. She had short blood-red hair pulled into a small bun on the right side of her head.

"Thank you," they chimed in unison.

CHAPTER 8

Jai, Arrow, and Cahya served themselves. Jai tasted the spicy rolls; they were hot and savory. He had never had anything like this before. So many flavors dancing on his tongue. His diet consisted mostly of eggs, beans, and rice back in Lower Ember. This meal was a true luxury.

"Arrow, how come Pyroceans have amber eyes and red hair?" Jai asked out of curiosity.

"Our eyes are amber as a result of living near a volcano. Our hair is blood red because of our dragon energy. Long ago, Pyroc was the land of the dragons, the great beasts. There were many kinds of dragons of varying sizes and appearances. Back then, only one dragon could fly and breathe fire. This was the DragonLord. This dragon had lived for thousands of years, thriving in a volcano guarding one egg that refused to hatch. As the Fireheart population grew, we needed more space. Hence, a Fireheart named Pyre set off to Pyroc to ask the DragonLord if Firehearts could settle on his land."

"Pyre's journey was difficult, and many dragons of varying abilities tried to stop him on his way to the DragonLord. They say that the DragonLord settled inside a dormant volcano. When Pyre reached the entrance, the DragonLord told him that he could not enter if he was scared of fire. Pyre told him he wasn't, and the DragonLord made his volcano active, spewing fiery lava. Pyre wasn't afraid and never left the volcano as the magma threatened to consume him. The dragon saw his passion for his cause and admired his bravery."

"The DragonLord ceased the eruption and allowed Pyre to enter the volcano. Pyre asked for land on behalf of the Firehearts. The DragonLord said that if he allowed that, dragons and humans would not coexist peacefully. He admitted to Pyre that a human from a WaterBearing tribe killed the mother of his only egg, and without its mother, it would not hatch. Pyre offered to use his fire to hatch the egg because the DragonLord's fire was too strong for the egg to handle and would have killed the offspring. When Pyre hatched the egg, the DragonLord gave his life to Pyre and infused his spirit into him. He told Pyre to tell the Firehearts of his journey and only return with those who believed in him."

"Pyre did just that, and a new Pyroc was taking birth. The other kinds of dragons followed the DragonLord's lead and infused their spirits into the Pyroceans. The dragons didn't die but took a new form within the souls of the Pyroceans. This power transfer caused the hair of the Pyroceans to become blood red. The color of the soul of the dragons. Pyre became the leader of Pyroc and raised the DragonLord's young hatchling to adulthood. When it became an adult, Pyre was one hundred years old, with two adult sons and several grandchildren."

"The young dragon told Pyre to pass the spirit of the DragonLord to his oldest son and bring the dragon to his younger son. Pyre did just that. When the younger son saw the dragon, it infused its spirit into him, creating a family with insurmountable dragon energy. Pyre built a palace for his sons close to the volcano where he met the DragonLord. Pyre's family became the family of the DragonLords," Arrow concluded the story.

"That's amazing! So you're the descendant of Pyre, the first Pyrocean," Cahya folded his arms. "Who would have thought that I would meet a Legend and a crown prince in my lifetime?"

"I am not a crown prince! It's Dragon Prince Asahi, son of the High Lord, brother of the DragonLord!"

"That's amazing. I guess Pyre is a popular name here," Jai guessed.

"Yes, as well as Bhasker and Asahi, Pyre's two sons," Arrow added as he continued eating.

"Pyre went through many tests to be worthy of the DragonLord's sacrifice and didn't flinch in the face of danger when his life was on the line when the volcano erupted. And he brought with him only those who believed in him, and they were the only ones ready to accept the spirit of the dragons. Wow, that's something," Jai reflected.

Pyre must have been a great leader worthy of the DragonLord's sacrifice. The choices Pyre made shaped the future of an entire people. Jai wanted to have an impact on people likened to Pyre. He wanted to be a Legend that left his people with a positive impact. Pyre's story made him want to make the most of his training with Sheraga.

After an hour, the trio had finished their food and was getting ready to sleep. Arrow, who seemed genuinely tired, fell asleep rather quickly. Cahya and Jai were wide awake.

Cahya looked up at the tall ceilings, "Are you going to be a better Legend than Cyra?"

"Uh, I guess. I still don't understand what is so bad about her."

"She betrayed her people by marrying a Waterbearer. She and Aenon started a war, and the world hasn't been the same since then. The Legends before them toppled many power-hungry people and secured a world of peace. Cyra and Aenon ruined the world. I don't understand what they were thinking! Like how can you be attracted to a Waterbearer? What did he have that she couldn't find in a Fireheart?"

"She made a mistake, Cahya. I am pretty sure that she did some good things in her life too."

"Maybe she did. But does it matter? After everything that has happened, does it matter? She wasn't a child; she knew better. She knew the Universal Order. Cyra came from a prestigious family and she damned their names. I don't know. Just don't fall in love with a Waterbearer. Or anyone who isn't a Fireheart."

"You don't have to worry about me."

Cahya yawned. "I'm not worried about you doing something so ridiculous. I hope I didn't annoy you with the whole Cyra thing. I was just curious. In all honesty, I've always wanted a brother, but I got stuck with Calida. I'm joking!"

"Really, Cahya!" Jai sighed before laughing. Cahya sat up and looked toward the window. "What are you looking for," Jai asked.

"I need to make sure the message was received." A few moments passed, and Cahya yawned again and said, "Now I can go to sleep."

"How did you know the message was received?"

"Dysis sent two lightning flashes. One flash means everything's fine, two means a message has been received, three means trouble, and a laser flash means a crisis situation. Everyone has scattered to safety locations. Dysis is such a powerful Fireheart; I really admire her," Cahya sighed.

"I don't know how you can be tired. The volcano is keeping me energized," Jai sighed.

"Don't let it energize you. Let it heat you up. Focus on the warmth, not the energy, and the warmth will send you to sleep," Cahya yawned again.

Jai tried to focus on the warmth radiating from the volcano. Still, it wasn't easy to separate the warmth from the energy. Maybe this was why everyone had been telling him to rest earlier. Perhaps it wasn't just the volcano keeping him awake. Yesterday he was a nobody, with no friends, no family other than his father figure, Arka. But that changed in the blink of an eye. He mattered to many people within twenty-four hours, forging friendships. The Universe had a unique destiny waiting for him. Only one thing was holding him back: the lack of skill and proficiency with his gift.

Could he really be a great Legend with such an unusual gift?

I'm not powerful. How could I ever stop a war?

He can't spew fire like every other Fireheart he has met. Jai believed everything he'd been told, and it wouldn't make sense that someone wanted him dead if he was a complete nobody. However, there was this fear he couldn't change anything. Can this guy from Lower Ember live up to the expectations of a Legend?

Could he really end the People's War? What did the Universe see in him? How was he worthy? Even though doubt threatened to consume his every thought, Jai reflected on Pyre. He didn't know what he was getting into when he first went to seek the DragonLord. His people had a problem, and he tried to fix it. He was driven and persistent and weathered many tests to achieve what he wanted: a place to call home.

Would fire and light be enough to end a war that started hundreds of years ago? Even though Jai didn't feel worthy, he wanted to try. He wanted to fight his doubts and disbelief and give his all to exceed the Firehearts' expectations. He was curious about Cyra of Kindle. Jai found it puzzling that Cahya asked him if he would be a better legend than her. Arrow had also mentioned that Cyra didn't do much of a service to the Firehearts. Jai hoped and prayed that he would do a better job for his people. He also wanted to know what she did that made her legacy bad. And if she was that bad, why would the Flamethrowers be so loyal to helping her successor? These thoughts swirled in his mind, making sleep difficult.

Jai turned these thoughts from his mind and focused on his beating heart. He reflected on everything he had gone through and promised himself that no matter what happened, he would be like Pyre and keep going. He pledged that he would always fight to be what his people needed. This settled the inner conflict he was experiencing, and a wave of peace rushed over him. Once he was calm, he began to finally drift off to sleep.

CHAPTER 9

The piercing rays of the sun gently pulled Jai from his slumber. At a bare minimum, he was coherent. Though the warmth felt wonderful, he didn't want to get up. This was the best sleep he had ever experienced. The palace beds were so comfortable; the weight of his body was enveloped in bliss. The atmosphere was peaceful. The commotion from robbery, violence, or the desperate cries of a child missing its family were absent here.

"Come on, man, the sun's up. Sheraga will be waiting for you outside," Arrow called. He was fully awake and rushing to make his bed.

Jai groaned, "I'm tired! Why is he up so early?"

"Come on now; you're a Fireheart. We rise with the sun. You'd rather me wake you than Sheraga. He has an impatient streak regarding training, and I'd hate for him to embarrass you because you made him wait," Arrow urged Jai. He sat up and got out of the bed. He saw Cahya sleeping peacefully on his stomach, face buried in his pillow.

"What about him? Is he even breathing?" Jai raised one brow.

"Who knows? The longer he sleeps, the better. He won't be awake to annoy me," Arrow smirked. "The washroom is outside to your right. You can't miss it."

Jai followed Arrow's instructions and quickly washed up. He ran his fingers through his black hair in a feeble attempt to look halfway presentable before Sheraga. After he washed, Arrow led him to the back of the palace. Double doors separated them from the outside, which looked like a stone patio.

Arrow opened the door for Jai, "Just do your best."

Jai nodded and walked through the doors. Sheraga's red hair was gently blowing through the wind. He was sitting on his knees, a red and gold robe dragging the ground around him.

Is he meditating?

Jai was unsure if the DragonLord wanted to be bothered and slowly turned on his heels to leave.

"You're finally awake," Sheraga said, never turning his head. His voice was low and controlled.

"Arrow got me up. I'm ready!"

"Are you sure?" Sheraga asked.

"Mhmm," Jai said without hesitating.

Sheraga stood and looked Jai in the eye. The intensity was unsettling; his eyes were such a bright amber, they looked bright orange in the sunlight. He hadn't yet been face to face with Sheraga—this gaze was nearly impossible to hold. The DragonLord raised a blood-red eyebrow, "So what are you waiting for? One mile ahead of us is a semi-active volcano. You'll have plenty of space to stretch your gift as far as possible."

"And you want me to do what now?"

"Show your gifts! Do something, anything," Sheraga seemed irritated by Jai's response.

"I don't know what's going to happen. I've never just let it out."

"Well, today that changes. Set it free."

Taking a deep breath, Jai opened his hands and let the light free. He didn't attempt to control it, and the light radiated like a second sun sitting on the earth. The feeling was liberating . . . and uncomfortable. Most people would be forced to turn away or avert their gaze, but Sheraga never even squinted. "All right, you're obviously comfortable with this form of your gift; now turn it into fire," Sheraga directed.

Jai focused on turning the light into fire, but nothing happened.

"Did you hear me?" Sheraga asked calmly.

"Yes, it's not doing it," Jai groaned.

"All right, you can stop." Sheraga clapped his hands, slowly walking over to where Jai stood, "Do you know what makes fire?"

Jai looked slightly puzzled. "Don't answer that," Sheraga smiled. "You're focused on the wrong thing. The light came easy to you because you weren't trying to make it happen. When I told you to transform it to a flame, your face started straining." Sheraga put his hands on his abdominal muscles, "Inhale and exhale. Do you feel that?"

Jai nodded, recognizing the presence of the muscles Sheraga was pointing out to him, "This is where you focus your thoughts. Fire is unique. Of all the gifts, fire is created internally. Therefore, you have to be the fire. Fire is passion and energy, and it's proactive, never passive. Take short, powerful breaths." Jai took several short breaths. "Do you feel your body heating up?"

Jai noticed that his abdominal muscles were warm. He nodded to Sheraga. "Now, focus on making a fist. Now, one of the most important things to know in learning this element is discipline. You have to guide that fire; if not, it will be wild and uncontrollable. People get hurt because of that. You must know exactly what you want the fire to do and where it will go. If you don't, you will never control it. Ignite the fire in your core, then focus on the heat coming only from the second finger in the fist, the middle knuckle. Now punch at me," he commanded. Jai made a fist and focused on the short breaths. He looked at Sheraga and punched at him. A magnificent flame extended from his fist toward Sheraga, which he dodged with extreme ease.

"Wow, who knew that breathing would make such a difference?" Jai marveled.

"Don't get too excited. Now that you know the technique, give me a hundred punches just like that. Turn to face the volcano, and if you miss one, you have to start all over."

Jai took a deep breath. He got into a fighting stance and began punching, counting to himself. He was amazed to see fire coming from his punches at a steady pace. Once he got to fifty, he missed one. He continued, thinking Sheraga would not notice, "Start all over. What? Did you think I was joking? Start again," Sheraga ordered, pacing back and forth.

He started again. This time he made it to ninety before missing one. "Start again," Sheraga demanded. Jai's arms were tired, but he took a deep breath and started again. It took him two more tries to reach one hundred; his arms trembled from exhaustion.

"Okay, that was progress. Now for kicks, the fire comes from the ball of the foot for a front kick and the side of the foot in a sidekick. You will need to pay closer attention to your core to keep your balance. As a Fireheart, gripping the ground with your toes is not our style. That is a Landkeeper technique, and it inhibits the distance that the flame can travel from your foot. However, in my study, I've learned that it is an excellent technique to teach fire kicks to a novice. I want you to grip the ground with your toes, only for balance. Then you will focus on achieving agility and speed, which will force you to stop gripping the ground. Don't bounce on your toes, though. That's a Windmaster technique and due to the difference in how our bodies are built, it's ineffective for us. Now show a front kick. Don't forget the breathing exercises. Remember, ignite the fire from your core."

After taking a deep breath, Jai was pleased to see fire extending from his kick. However, he was gripping the ground. The kicks were an unnatural feeling for him. As a blacksmith, he was accustomed to using his arms. It was much easier to feel himself with the punches. He felt like an ungraceful animal feverishly struggling for balance as he kicked. Sheraga then challenged him to kick with one leg and punch with the opposite hand.

He wants me to get the agility and speed and stop grounding myself.

Sheraga explained that he had to do two hundred without missing one. After an hour, Jai felt like he could barely stand anymore. He was losing control over his muscles, and his body was trembling from exhaustion.

Holy Stars! This must be what they meant!

Sheraga was pacing back and forth, and he knew immediately whenever Jai missed one. He started over for the seventh time. This time Jai counted every rep. He didn't want to fall out as Suvan had said. He focused on the story Arrow had told him of Pyre and imagined every punch was a step Pyre had to take on his journey to the DragonLord. The strategy was working. He forgot about his fatigue and continued. He didn't miss one punch or kick.

Sheraga lightly punched his shoulder, "Good! Most would have fallen to their knees begging for a break by now."

Jai mumbled. His arms and legs were burning.

"Now, we spar," Sheraga smiled as he pulled his long hair into a ponytail.

No way in fiery hell! Spar?! He's lost his mind! He's been pacing around and I'm beat!

"What! I thought that meant I was getting a break!"

"Have you ever been to war?"

"No."

"Been in a battle or skirmish?"

Jai shook his head no.

"Well here's the thing: there are no breaks in war, and because of that, I don't give breaks. You did pretty well. You're quite gifted, but you lose what you don't use. You have to use your gift. You must fall in love, adore, and play with it. And you're trying to make up for lost time. Most Firehearts have a complete handle on all of their abilities at your age. So the additional practice will be beneficial. Now, no fire. I want to see your fighting skills."

Sheraga got into a fighting stance; he showed off the same punch and kick combination he had Jai to do in double time. After a rigorous display of fiery punches and kicks, Sheraga never broke a sweat. Jai's body trembled, but suddenly the doors opened.

"I hope I'm not creating a disturbance," a slightly raspy voice said. Jai turned to face the speaker and was pleasantly shocked by what he saw—an unusual-looking woman. She stood two inches taller than Sheraga, who was two inches taller than him. Her skin was the color of warm brown sugar cubes, and her eyes were a striking silver. Her cheekbones were high and her lips full. Her steel-colored hair had a braided crown with a medium-sized bun toward the back adorned with a silver hairpin containing a yellow jewel drop. Her slim build was lightly muscled. Her top was a soft yellow and would have probably been flowy if it was not tucked into high-waisted gray harem pants. She wore charcoal leather flats that covered most of her foot, while her hands were covered in steel mesh gloves. The gloves made a unique contrast with the skin of her hands. There was a circular blade attached to a loop on her pants. Jai was in awe of her appearance. She was an unusual woman, beautiful from every angle.

"Sheraga, Aqila is here," Arrow introduced the pretty girl. Jai had not taken his eyes off her. And likewise, she never took her eyes off him.

"Jai, we are finished for the day." Sheraga pulled his hair free from his ponytail. "Aqila, this is Jai. This is Aqila; she's a seer."

"Apprentice seer, Sheraga," Aqila corrected. "This is intriguing, the golden-eyed Legend. What a turn of events," she walked around him. Her eyes were so bright and intense that Jai almost had to look away.

"I thought you were here for me," Sheraga said.

Aqila turned her head to Sheraga, "I requested a private audience with you in order to give you an important message."

"Go ahead, Storm. I don't have anything to hide from anyone," Sheraga replied in a nonchalant tone. Curious, Arrow leaned on the door frame, and Jai decided to sit on the stone ground. He caught Arrow's eye; he was holding back laughter.

"It's not good news. Agni is planning to make a concentrated attack on Pyroc before the month is out. He claims that Pyroc has created multiple problems for Lower Ember and has a track record of aggression near the border. It's a dire situation. He has secured complete satisfaction in Lower Ember and is also trying to get support from Upper Ember. However, he's not gaining much traction there, thanks to Sitara's efforts. Agni has won favor in Lower Ember, and the citizens there are willing to follow his every order to the letter. Sheraga, he's going to bring the war to Pyroc."

"And?" Aqila shook her head in disbelief. "Don't answer that." He continued, "Okay, so he wants war—he'll get one. Pyroc's army is larger than the entire Lower Ember. What do I need to worry about?" Sheraga offered her a smug smile and shrugged his shoulders.

"You have an inside scoop, and you're going to sit on it?" Aqila raised her long steel-colored eyebrows.

"Did you have a vision?" Sheraga asked.

"Are you kidding me?"

"Dodging questions, little lady?"

"Of course not! And I'm not little!"

"Not in size but in the age department, I think I'm stacked with the larger number."

"Stop trying to change the subject!"

"Did you have a vision?"

"He's leading a cult!"

"Vision?"

Aqila sighed, "No, I didn't."

"Okay then, so I'm not going to attack first. What kind of DragonLord would I be if I solely ran on hunches?"

"I know what I saw! The headquarters! I saw where he's headquartered! He has Lower Ember in the palm of his hand! He is manipulating those poor souls! And their living conditions are so subpar that Agni's cult seems to be promising, and they will back him!"

Sheraga raised a hand to silence her. "But I will obliterate his so-called forces if they take one step into my land. Sound fair, little lady?"

"You don't want to know why? There is always a why! I know why! We are literally looking at the reason why," Aqila pointed to Jai frantically.

"Me?"

"Yes, you!"

"What on earth are you talking about?" Sheraga huffed, growing annoyed with the apprentice.

"It's simple. Agni has been cooking up problems for a while. It doesn't matter if Lower Ember doesn't see it that way. Hello! He has single-handedly created a divide between Lower Ember and Pyroc, then between Upper Ember and Kindle. Why? To distract everyone from the real motive, finding Jai! Now, suddenly, he wants to fight Pyroc while Jai is here. That's not a coincidence. Agni knows who the Legend is and wants him out of the way. And to top it off, I can tell you the general vicinity of Agni's secret headquarters that I semi-saw in a vision. It's on the border of Upper and Lower Ember. There's a new little town of houses along the border line, it's right around there!" Aqila beamed with pride.

"That does make sense with the information the Flamethrowers have been collecting. Sheraga, she's not lying," Arrow supported Aqila.

"I didn't ask for your opinion. And I didn't say that she was lying. I'm just not pressed about someone wanting to fight Pyroc. We would blow them to the end of the Universe, far beyond the domain of the Stars, with no problem at all," Sheraga boasted.

Aqila lowered her head and sighed, "Like my mentor, Zeroun, would say, 'All you can do is relay the message.'"

"Whatever. It would be different if you were telling me about a vision you had, a real vision. Storm, I'm not brushing you off. I'm just not concerned about an attack. Pyroc has the greatest military in the world right now, and I plan on keeping it that way. However," he walked over to her, looking up to meet her gaze, "I appreciate having an apprentice seer as my valued ally."

A blaring screech made Jai cover his ears. Aqila snatched Sheraga by the collar, "Your violent-tempered beast better not touch a feather on my Talon." With that, Aqila darted off with unbelievable speed.

Sheraga laughed heartily, straightening out his collar, "That girl and her bird."

"Sheraga, shouldn't you check to make sure that Ash isn't harassing Talon? Ash has a venomous bite." Arrow questioned his brother's humor.

The DragonLord rolled his eyes and spoke to Jai, "You did average today. Nothing impressive, but I've seen worse. If you want, we can continue tomorrow morning. I want you to do one hundred fire punches and kicks before arriving to continue our lesson. We will work on fighting techniques tomorrow. Arrow, tell Aqila congratulations on behalf of the DragonLord family."

Jai nodded, and Sheraga left, heading in the direction Aqila darted in moments before.

"I was shocked when she grabbed him like that," Jai admitted to Arrow.

"Those two go at it all the time. There's nothing to worry about. Aqila travels here a lot. She's like a family friend. I think she's around your age. I'm two years older than both of you," Arrow smiled.

"I wonder how tall she is."

"She's about six foot five; very bold, but quite friendly."

"She's that tall!"

"Yeah, all Windmasters are tall. The average Windmaster man's height is over seven feet," Arrow replied. Jai's eyes went wide.

"Seven feet, three inches to be exact," Aqila returned with a bird nearly the size of the hut they stayed in the other night.

Aqila saw Jai's expression. "This is my dasher. His name is Talon, and he's a great gray owl. Strix nebulosa, to be exact."

"I've never seen a bird that big before," Jai was in awe as he stepped closer to her dasher. His eyes went wide as the owl flapped and squawked.

"Most birds aren't this large. However, in Kashmala and Wyndhm, eagles, owls, and hawks grow to incredible sizes. We domesticate them for riding."

"You ride that?" Jai gasped.

"Yes, that's how she got here. This guy can handle carrying three or four people," Arrow chimed in. "I hope Ash wasn't being a pain. Congrats on behalf of the family."

"He was, as usual, thrashing his tail at Talon like that," Aqila petted the giant face of her bird and peppered him in kisses. "And thank you," she whispered, smiling to herself.

"Ash is Sheraga's Komodo dragon. He's a little aggressive," Arrow whispered to Jai.

"Aqila, you have visions?" Jai asked.

"Yeah, I wouldn't be a seer to any degree if I didn't."

"Could you try and see what Agni wants with me and why I'm important to him?"

"Sight doesn't work like that, and it takes a lot of mental effort to get a full vision. The sight is a gift from the Universe, and I need a peaceful environment and the right conditions, including additional information. Things like that."

"Would you try?" Jai asked.

"If I could, I would, but I'm an apprentice seer, and I have to wait for the sight sensation to claim me. My mentor, Zeroun, now he can have visions under the proper conditions if you ask him. I wish I was more help, but if a vision comes to me about you or Agni, you can trust that I'll inform you."

"Aqila, you said that you did have a vision that his headquarters was on the Upper and Lower Ember line, right?" Arrow asked.

Aqila nodded, "I really think he knows about you."

"I do, too. I just want to know why he's trying to kill me," Jai replied.

Aqila sensed the mood turning dreary, "What do you have planned for the day?"

"Um, nothing," Jai hesitated.

"Let's hang out!"

She seems like a big ball of energy. This may be fun.

"Okay," Jai replied, "what do you want to do? I've wanted to explore Pyroc since I've been here."

"Wait a minute! Aqila, you just said that Agni is planning an attack here and probably wants to kill Jai, and you want to run around and hang out?!" Arrow was borderline furious.

"Not to be rude, but Sheraga's in charge here, and he's not concerned. I did my part. Now, I want to enjoy my time and get an opportunity to experience the golden-eyed Legend for myself. And if the sight comes to me, he'll be right there!"

"I don't know, Aqila. The Flamethrowers are taking responsibility for his well-being," Arrow shook his head.

"Not to be rude again, but there's nothing you need to know," she said, walking toward him, her face hovering over his. "Jai is not a child. You're not responsible for his well-being. You're his loyal followers; there's a difference. So back up and let him breathe. Nothing's going to happen to him on my watch. I know you don't think you'd do a better job at ensuring his safety than I could. I hate to bring this up, but I can beat you and your four

Flamethrowers in a fight without breaking a sweat. If it came down to that," Aqila gave Arrow a friendly smile. "Jai, I'll be at the front of the palace when you're ready." She sat on Talon, and together they flew off.

A bold woman indeed. She handles Sheraga and Arrow like they're nothing at all.

"Wow, she's intense, but I like her," Jai exclaimed.

"Yeah, she's a powerful Windmaster. She's technically stronger than us five Flamethrowers combined. She's right. Fire is freedom. You have the freedom to explore Pyroc as you'd like. Sorry, I tend to get wound up when I'm protective. I'll head off to catch the Flamethrowers up. Enjoy yourself, Jai." Arrow humbly walked back inside.

Jai ran around the side of the palace, hurrying to the front to meet Aqila.

CHAPTER 10

When Jai arrived, he saw Aqila casually talking with the off-duty soldiers. Everyone seemed engaged, talking and laughing. When she saw him, she waved, motioning for him to come ride on her dasher.

"Sorry to abruptly end our conversation, but I promised I'd take the Legend sightseeing. I'll come again soon," Aqila explained. The soldiers groaned that she had to go.

Jai awkwardly climbed on Talon and sat behind Aqila. The back of the bird felt strange.

If we're flying, what am I going to hold onto? Her? This could get awkward . . .

"I don't normally use a riding mat, but you may find that more comfortable." They both dismounted, and she grabbed the mat from a substantially sized carry bag strapped to Talon's side. She placed the long mat on Talon's back, fastening its straps on the side. It was designed for up to three people. There was a mount for their feet and a handlebar for the second and third riders.

Now, I can work with that!

Aqila remounted and motioned for Jai to do the same.

"Wow, that feels comfortable. You say you don't use the mat?" Jai asked, surprised that she preferred bareback riding.

"Yeah, not often. I learned to ride without it," Talon took off slowly and flew about a mile above the ground. "If you feel uncomfortable, let me know. I can have Talon hover instead," She glanced back at him.

"No, this is amazing. I feel so close to the sun," Jai replied, basking in the sun's welcoming rays. "Where are you from?"

"Kashmala; how about you?"

"Lower Ember, I've only heard of Kashmala. Everyone says it's nice there."

"It really is. I miss it a lot," Aqila said, glancing back.

"How come? Don't you live there?"

"Yeah, in a way. I live in a mountain home on the tallest eastern peak. I haven't been in Kashmala, the state, in a while."

"Why not?"

"I'll have been an apprentice seer for ten years in a few months. I live with my mentor. Before that, I lived with my guardian in Kashmala and went to school there until I was ten."

"You're turning twenty soon; I turn twenty this month!"

"Neat! We were born the same year," she looked back, smiling at him.

"Becoming a seer must take a lot of commitment. Do you like it? Is it hard work?" Jai asked.

"It's like any kind of occupation: there are things you love and things you wish were different. Sight takes a lot of mental effort and can be draining. And preparing for visions requires much study."

He felt Talon landing. "Where are we going?"

"I want to show you one of my favorite places," she beamed excitedly. Aqila said something to Talon, and he screeched back. "Let's go!" They walked for several minutes through the streets of Pyroc. There was a strong military atmosphere throughout the town in addition to the constant bustle of activity and noise. The front doors of the homes were adorned with ornate carvings and paintings depicting warriors and battles.

Jai could smell food as Aqila led him past a market. The smells of grilled meat, fresh vegetables, and sweet citrus filled the air, mixed with the pungent aroma of horses and armor. The noise was deafening, with the clanging of metal, the whinnying of horses, and the constant chatter of merchants trying to sell their wares. Walking further into the town, they saw numerous training grounds where young warriors honed their skills with flame and weapons. The sound of metal clashing against metal could be heard from every corner, as these warriors engaged in mock battles to prepare themselves for war.

As they slowed to a stop, Jai saw a large sign, "Flame Eaters." This was probably where they were going.

"Here we are," she opened the flap entrance to an arena. "It's an acrobatic show, and this group is called the Flame Eaters. Did you know that the Windmasters introduced aerial acrobatics to the Firehearts? This place reminds me of home a bit. That's why I like coming here."

"No, I didn't know that. I've never seen acrobatics before. Funny, it's kind of a dream job for young people in Lower Ember. When was the first time you came here?"

"With Zeroun—it was my first week after I moved to the mountain home. He brought me here and gave me a spicy rock candy. The first one was too hot for me, then he gave me a hot chocolate one, and I could handle that," she smiled when talking about her mentor.

It warmed Jai's heart and made him think about Arka. Not for long, however, as the light dimmed when the acrobats arrived. Their costumes were incredible. Red and orange were the dominant colors. But there were lovely shades of purple, teal, and gold. Jewels, glitter, and feathers embellished the clothes worn by the performers. Jai was completely in awe of the scene. He could understand why anyone would want to leave Lower Ember to be a part of this.

The arena was dead silent—not an uncomfortable silence, though. Several more acrobats entered the arena, and the show began. Jai was amazed at the men and women doing intricate flips and twirls. There were people doing stunts through hoops of fire. One man performed flips on a burning trapeze. And there was a woman doing flips between lightning bolts.

One young woman was spinning through the air by her ponytail, spewing fire as she turned. The fire lit the arena with a brilliant warmth. The act seemed otherworldly. Looking at Aqila from the corner of his eye, he could see how she was enjoying the show. The fire made the pretty yellow jewel hanging from her hairpin glisten in its light and refract into more glorious colors.

"Yes?" she whispered, never looking at him.

"The hairpin. It's beautiful," Jai looked away. He wished Arrow was there to have reminded him that it was rude to stare.

"Thank you," she murmured with a smile on her face. "You don't want to miss this part," she pointed to the man standing on the ground, spitting fire from his mouth. The audience cheered him on. Suddenly, he roared, and a massive dragon made purely of fire erupted from his mouth. The man danced around the dragon, sometimes barely dodging the flames. Jai's mouth went agape. It was almost as if the dragon was alive and had a mind of its own. The act continued until the dragon flew up and raced around the arena, coming within feet of the audience.

Clapping and cheering followed. The dragon appeared to have all of its features constructed with fire. The heat was intense. If anyone got too close, the flames would singe their eyebrows, reducing them to nothing. Nonetheless, Jai found this part of the show to be the best. The man who breathed the dragon then ate the dragon flames, earning a standing ovation from the audience.

After the dragon flames, the show was over. "That was amazing, Aqila. I can see why you like it so much," Jai was impressed.

Then, walking through the Pyrocean town, Aqila whistled at Talon, and he began to hover above them. "What kinds of things do you like?"

Jai was surprised by Aqila's question, "Um, I like simple things. Comfy bed, sunny days, hot scrambled eggs, things like that." Aqila nodded in response. She calmly walked through the town. Some people acknowledged her presence, a few even asking her to give them a vision. She was friendly to all. Jai had unintentionally been staring at her when she asked, "Yes?"

"Sorry, I don't mean to stare. I've never met a Windmaster."

Aqila giggled, "I can tell. You can ask me questions, you know."

"What's that circular thing on your belt?"

"It's a wind blade. It's more of a shield, its edges are sharp enough to use as a weapon, but the purpose of the blade is to slice or deflect approaching objects. But since it is sharp, it has to be handled with these mesh gloves."

"I was curious about that from the moment I saw you. That's very different from the traditional sword or dagger. What's your family like?"

"What do you mean?"

"Like your parents? Do you have any brothers or sisters?"

"I don't know," she shrugged her shoulders.

"What's that supposed to mean?"

"I never met my parents, so I wouldn't know if I had siblings," Aqila replied.

"I'm sorry—" Jai hung his head.

"It's fine. I was born during Mercury in transit when the planet comes in between the sun and the earth. A Windmaster born during the peak of that event is destined to be a seer. Like the seers before me, my parents gave up their guardianship to allow me to be raised by the community until I was a full seer. I am a public servant to my people. In Kashmala and Wyndhm, I belong to everyone. I will meet my parents once I become a full seer. I am proud that they made a mighty sacrifice for the good of our people. I just have to do my part. I've been told that I am my parents' firstborn. I can't imagine what they endured; I refuse to let their sacrifice be in vain."

"That's unbelievable. I hope you become a full seer soon," Jai smiled.

"Thanks, so do I. Then I can give people the visions they ask for," Aqila smiled back at him. "How is your training going? If you're staying at the palace, I guessed Sheraga was training you. So how's that been?"

Everyone seems so curious about my training.

"I felt like my arms and legs were going to fall off! But he's showing me some helpful techniques. Now I know how to generate fire. I use light manipulation, but until today I couldn't generate fire."

"How does it feel?"

"The light feels great; the fire I'm still a little uncomfortable with."

"Why?"

"I don't know."

"Maybe trying to understand the why will help you get more comfortable with your gift."

"Perhaps. I've never thought about why. The light comes so naturally. While the fire just feels so forced."

"As a Windmaster, we are encouraged to always think about the reason why something occurs. It promotes deeper thinking, allowing one to arrive at a complete truth. What do you like about the light?"

"I have always loved the light because it was so beautiful. Now that I can use it for healing major wounds, I appreciate it more. Eww, I sound like a Waterbearer."

"Is there something wrong with that?"

"Yeah, my natural enemy of sorts. But nothing really wrong with it. Honestly, I love healing. I was a blacksmith in Lower Ember. I would get little cuts and burns all the time. I'd apply just a touch of light, and I'd be good as new. Recently, I revived a dead person by applying the light to the fatal wound. I had never done that before!"

"Maybe you already know why. The light nurtures and protects, and you love the healing properties that it holds. Fire requires passion and an unbreakable drive to chase your passions. It's aggressive, forward, and proactive. The light is vibrant, powerful, and yet nurturing. Have you noticed that you are not as outgoing, wild, or rambunctious as the average Fireheart?"

"I've noticed that I'm very calm compared to the average gifted Fireheart. I feel like it's bound to be a problem on my journey as a Legend. Looking at other Firehearts, I'm so weak. Fiery hell, even those Flame Eaters were packing more skills than me!"

Talon landed softly, and the pair mounted. "You want me to tell you about your predecessor, Cyra?"

"YES! Everyone's been beating around the bush when talking about her, but I want to know more." Together they flew through the warm air of the Pyrocean skies. In the distance, they could see a semi-active volcano, its rugged slopes and jagged peaks rising from the earth. As they drew closer, the details of the volcano became clearer. Smoke and steam billowed from the crater, creating a halo of mist around the summit. The rocks on the slopes were black and barren. Jai couldn't help but be mesmerized by the volcano's raw power and majesty. The pair eventually landed near the top of the semi-active volcano behind the palace.

"Aqila, isn't this a bit dangerous?"

"Not at all: you're a Fireheart, and if the worst happens, Talon will get us." She said something to Talon, and he flew to the volcano's base. They walked up a few feet, nearing the top, when Aqila sat down with legs folded.

Jai sat down beside her. "This is a nice view of Pyroc."

"I know. I thought you'd like it. You can even see the palace soldiers doing drills in the distance. So you wanted to know about Cyra?"

"Mhmm," Jai nodded.

"Well, she was born in Kindle to prestigious Firehearts. Her mother was able to wield white fire, while her father trained in the Pyrocean military. They both earned many honors, increasing their status. Her parents did what they could to give their golden-eyed daughter a normal childhood. However, she found being accepted by the Firehearts difficult because she, like you, had a hard time using the flame. This brought her much shame. Because she had golden eyes, she didn't have the choice to exchange fire for lightning. She was able to alternate between the two abilities. She went to school and many masters trained her. However, none could help her master the flame. When she turned eighteen, Cyra journeyed to Pyroc. A military family who didn't have children allowed her to stay with them. The man of the house was an experienced soldier, and he trained her for ten years."

"Ten years? I hope it doesn't take me that long," Jai mumbled.

"Pyroc had just come out of a war around that time, and he was diligent in training Cyra. The flame didn't feel natural to her. However, she tried her best. At the end of ten years, Cyra's training made her a powerful combat soldier, despite not mastering fire. She served in the Pyrocean military as a general for two years before leaving. She journeyed to the Waterbearer Beach tribe and met Aenon. He recognized that she was the golden-eyed Legend. Eventually he revealed that he was also a Legend, born during the peak of the lunar eclipse. They became good friends, finding that they shared something in common. He asked her about her intentions as a Legend. Cyra was so focused on learning the flame that she never focused on her purpose. As the Fireheart, other Legends would look to her as they agreed on their purpose."

Gazing down on Pyroc, Aqila continued, "Cyra, at this time, had known Aenon for a year. She knew that the Firehearts and Waterbearers weren't on good terms, so she decided that she wanted all the earth's people to be one. She wanted to erase the boundaries that separated them. Aenon had come to like Cyra, more than as just a friend, and agreed to her idea of a new earth. They spent the next year traveling together, looking for the other two Legends. They eventually found Basir and his close friend, Ila. Basir and Ila had met as teenagers. He was 'The One Who Knows.' The Stars had already revealed to him that he was a Legend at an early age. Still, he couldn't reveal that knowledge to anyone until the others had recognized themselves to be Legends. Ila realized that she was a Legend when she was born with a new ability for the Landkeepers—the ability to use metal. She was isolated for her unusual ability and found friendship in Basir, who frequently traveled in search of other Legends.

"Basir had looked for the other Legends many times before. But since Aenon had not recognized his calling until much later in life, and Cyra traveled a lot herself, it took Basir much longer to find them. Basir revealed his identity as a Legend and the One Who Knew. Cyra told Basir and Ila about her and Aenon's plans for a new earth. Basir strongly disagreed. He told them that some elements could not coexist in the same space without destroying each other, like fire and water, air and earth. This is the foundation of why the Universe gave separate gifts that reflected the character and personality of those gifted. Cyra and Aenon challenged Basir and Ila to a fight to see whose point would stand. Basir found their reasoning illogical and decided not to fight them, to Ila's dismay."

"What did Cyra and Aenon do next?" Jai questioned.

"They declared Basir their enemy," Aqila answered. "Ila decided to shun them in support of her friend. Cyra and Aenon worked to force the Firehearts and Waterbearers to open borders, which only resulted in greater tensions. The pair got married. And one year later they had twin girls, but their daughter's eyes were brown, dark brown. The Universe did not gift their children. Aenon realized this was punishment for disobeying a Universal law—"

"No intermarrying of elements. Come on, that's a basic natural law. He had to have known that," Jai finished her sentence.

"Exactly. Aenon left Cyra and went back to his tribe. Cyra was hurt and angry. She felt like a failure. She stopped trying to make the people one but focused on keeping fire and water from a war. She went through many trials and suffered much pain and loss. Cyra single-handedly catapulted the war between the two peoples of fire and water. Years later, after the unfortunate deaths of Ila and Aenon, Cyra and Basir worked together to stop the People's War that they all had a hand in starting. Cyra's predecessor came to her in a dream, telling her to find and follow the light that was always inside of her—Lightning, the flash of light in the darkness. The moment she stopped being true to her ability and Universal gift was the beginning of her downfall. She prayed to the Universe for forgiveness and promised to reclaim the light and power of her own fire. The lightning was her unique fire type. She and Basir then agreed to change the goal by creating a home for all people and by understanding why the Universe sets boundaries."

Aqila continued, "My mentor said that Cyra and Basir worked the rest of their lives trying to restore order, but by that time, fire and water were at war, as well as earth and air. The Windmasters defeated the Landkeepers and isolated themselves from the other nations. Then the Landkeepers started having internal issues that eventually led to the civil war they are still in today. Some people have eased tensions while others have escalated. It's a mess, but the most important thing now is that you are here. A sign that the Universe is still trying to fix us."

"Wow, and that was the short version. Arrow told me that the previous Legends did a greater disservice than anything. I wasn't expecting that. What happened to Ila and Aenon?"

"After Aenon left Cyra, he went home and tried to help the struggling Snow Tribe. He married the queen. He and Basir gave the Snow Tribe a home, a mountain chain that belonged to the Windmasters. Then sometime later, he and Cyra had a heated argument when one of their twin daughters died trying to visit him. His new wife killed him because Cyra was completely melting their home in a fit of violent anger. Basir accidentally killed Ila. She made the metal-infused mountain chain that is Kashmala today. They argued about the fate of the Legends. They exchanged words and fought on top of the mountains. Ila got injured as Basir lost control of his power, and he absent-mindedly pushed her off a ledge. It was too late for Ila when he calmed down and realized what he had done. He spent three years in complete isolation until the Universe sent a sign that he had been forgiven. During his isolation, Cyra and Aenon had their final confrontation. Then Cyra and Basir made peace and worked to turn things around."

"Being a Legend isn't easy," Jai whispered.

"I guess not. But I told you that for a reason. Stay true to what feels right to you. If the light feels right, use it. Turn it into fire when it feels right. You'll have to play with it and get to know it intimately. The Universe gave you this unique gift for a reason. The Universe gives us what we need. You're equipped with everything you need to be successful. It's your job to find how to best utilize what you've been given."

"You're going to be a great seer. I don't know how you knew I needed to hear that, but I did. I was getting so focused on how other people were using their fire that I forgot that I had something completely new in mine. Thanks, Aqila," Jai patted her back and smiled at her.

"Anytime. I'm starting to feel a little more heat from this volcano. Let's meet Talon at the bottom." The pair stood and proceeded to where Talon diligently stood, waiting for his rider.

Aqila got on Talon's back, "You coming?"

"I'm so close to the palace, I'll walk, but thanks," Jai replied.

"All right, Talon needs to hunt, so I'm off. I hope to see you around. I'll be in Pyroc for another day, then I'm visiting one of my best friends in Theyra."

"You have a Landkeeper friend?"

"Yeah, his parents own this massive library that Zeroun often took me to. I have seven books to return, and I don't want to be docked for late books," she giggled. "Let the Universe guide your path, and you're bound to find greatness!" Talon flew her high into the sky as she shouted well wishes to him.

Jai waved at his new friend. It was late afternoon, and he started back to the palace. His mind was filled with Aqila's voice. She had this strange sensation about her; she seemed so wise and powerful. He hoped they would meet again soon. He was met at the back of the palace by Liora.

"Good to see you back, Jai. I know you had to enjoy yourself with Aqila. She's truly an adventurer," she laughed, opening the back double doors.

"Yeah, it was fun. I can't remember ever having such a good time, and I can't help but feel like I'd known her for a long time."

"Most Windmasters are generally friendly. Aqila is no exception. I'll let Sheraga know you're back. Your friends are waiting in your room, and Baara will bring some food soon."

CHAPTER 11

Jai went to the washroom before going back to Arrow's room. He washed his face and his hair too. About twenty minutes later, with damp hair, he entered the room. The Flamethrowers were sitting in the room with a space left for him between Arrow and Cahya.

"You're back," Arin exclaimed, excitement dancing in her honey-colored eyes. He couldn't help but feel unlike himself as he watched Arin's eyes linger on him for just a moment longer than necessary. It was as if Arin was trying to convey something to him, something that couldn't be put into words.

Cahya wiggled his eyebrows, "I know you had a good time with the Windmaster. I've heard Aqila is quite easy on the eyes."

"Cahya! She's a Windmaster!" Calida groaned and rolled her eyes.

"We were waiting for you to come back so we could all eat together, Jai," Arin meekly smiled at him.

"I hope I didn't keep you waiting too long," Jai replied, looking outside the massive window. It was late afternoon, and the sun was beginning its descent.

"No, we were just talking about the next steps," Calida continued.

Next steps for what? My training?

"I want to know about Aqila," Cahya demanded.

"Chill out! She's engaged and not to you," Arrow rolled his eyes.

"She's engaged? She didn't mention that." Jai was puzzled.

"Of course. That's what the hairpin is for. It's the traditional engagement gift for Windmasters. That's why Sheraga had me send her congratulations from our family," Arrow explained.

"Who's the lucky man?" Cahya asked. He was clearly interested in Aqila's personal life.

"All you need to know is that he's very tall and astute. Two things you are not," Arrow retorted to Cahya.

"How was your training, Jai?" Arin asked.

"Just as everyone warned, it was intense. I thought my arms were going to fall off. This guy takes no breaks! I had to do seven sets of fire kicks with alternating punches to get to the number he wanted. When I finally finished, I thought I would fall to my knees. Then Sheraga said, 'Let's spar!' However, Aqila came and saved the day."

Arrow laughed, "I told you: my brother has no chill regarding anything war related. You should have seen him. The second Aqila started talking, Jai sat down. I almost felt bad for you … almost. Rather you than me."

"So, on a serious note, what are we going to do about Agni? Arrow told me what Aqila said as well as how Sheraga responded. Suvan sent a note yesterday confirming Aqila's information. She's right. Somehow Agni knows about Jai," Calida explained. Her tone commanded everyone's attention.

"I want to know what he wants so bad that he's willing to go to war to get it," Jai answered.

"He isn't just willing to go to war; he's willing to kill you, Jai. Shouldn't you finish your training first?" Arin questioned. Concern was evident in her voice.

"Yeah, aren't you supposed to find your team . . . or your team is supposed to find you or something?" Alena added.

"No, we have to listen to Jai. He's the Legend, not us," Arrow reminded them.

"Jai, Agni has influence and an entire state within his control. Confronting him while you don't have good control over your gift doesn't seem sound," Calida echoed everyone's concern.

Arrow sighed and shook his head. "Jai, whatever you decide, I support. We all will."

"I know, and I promise I will do my part. I'm so glad that I met Aqila. She gave me the boost I needed by telling me a little about the previous Legends. I feel better about using my gift now. I will continue training but don't want a war to come to Pyroc because I'm here. The Firehearts have gone through enough war as it is," Jai asserted. The rest of the Flamethrowers looked at each other and then back to Jai, then nodded in agreement. Some seemed to accept his words more than others. Arrow wanted him to decide, but Calida seemed to already have a plan. The twins appeared to accept his stance; however, Cahya looked uneasy about whether to support Jai or his sister.

Baara slowly entered with a large tray of food cutting the growing tension in the room, "Thank you, Baara," Arrow acknowledged. Everyone nodded and murmured their thanks. As Baara left, the group began to eat. Cahya kept looking toward the window, "I'm going outside for a minute," he spoke absent-mindedly.

"Okay," Calida shrugged her shoulders. As she leaned over to eat, Jai noticed a thin chain around her neck. It had a gold band attached. It looked rather large for her relatively small hands. Jai assumed it may have been a gift from Arrow. The pair were close, and it was obvious to anyone with eyes that they were pretty fond of each other.

"Jai, what was Aqila like? Did she have any visions?" Alena asked excitedly.

"She was amazing and beautiful! She's so tall, even taller than Sheraga. Her eyes are bright, silverish in color, and her hair is a soft shade of gray. She dressed differently than I've ever seen, but all in all, she was really friendly. To be honest, for some reason, it seemed like we had known each other for a long time. I can't explain it. She didn't have any visions, though, but she did say that if she did, she'd let me know. Just for that, I'm grateful."

"I've heard a lot about her, but I've never met her myself. I heard that she is also extremely powerful," Calida chimed in.

"I could feel that in her presence. When she grabbed Sheraga's collar because his dragon was messing with her bird, my heart almost stopped. She is a bold woman," Jai chuckled.

"Rumor has it that she was born during a tornado or something. She's a Storm, and you wouldn't want to mess with her. Rumor or not, she is not to be trifled with," Arrow confirmed.

"What's a Storm?" Jai was puzzled.

"A Windmaster that was born during a storm, specifically a tornado or a hurricane. Their physical strength surpasses the physical strength of most Windmasters. And it marks their personalities. Windmasters are known for their laid-back and relaxed nature. Storms tend to be a lot more forward and oftentimes come off as aggressive," Arrow explained.

That makes so much sense! I could feel that boldness in everything she said and did.

"The concept started two Legend cycles ago with a Windmaster Legend named Storm. Her history is quite fascinating. She was born to an outcast clan and was exiled from the Windmasters because her nature conflicted with the way of wind. However, she ended up being the perfect ally of the Fireheart Legend Lio. She eventually returned to her people and created the WindGuard, allowing the Windmasters to step into the future and assert for themselves a strong and powerful territory. The Windmasters would have lost the war with the Landkeepers if it wasn't for Storm establishing a military. Sorry, got carried away," Arrow said.

"Wouldn't that create some problems?" Alena asked. "They would be stronger than the other Windmasters, so how did everyone else respond?"

Arrow smiled. "In Kashmala and Wyndhm, physical strength doesn't matter as much as mental prowess. The Windmasters' objective is to outsmart and outmaneuver their opponents. Being physically strong is a little perk, but not a big deal to them. Trust me, Aqila is the full package: brains, brawn, and beauty."

"I'm going to go check on Cahya," Arin smiled gently and stood to leave.

"Arin, wait! Aren't you gonna finish your food?" Alena asked, "Or did those candies spoil your appetite?"

"I think I did have too many candies, but I'm fine. I'll be back soon," Arin gently closed the door behind her.

"Hope she's okay," Calida murmured.

Everyone shrugged off Arin's exit—everyone except Jai.

Is it just me or did she seem a little uncomfortable? Was it the conversation?

After everyone finished eating, Calida and Alena left to go to their shared room. Arrow plopped onto his bed. "What's up?"

"Nothing. Why do you ask?" Jai replied as he headed toward the window.

"Seems like everybody is starting to act all strange. First Cahya, then Arin, and now you. I just wanted to know if something was bothering you," Arrow explained, running his hands through his blood-red hair.

"I mean, I wouldn't say that anything is bothering me. I just have a lot of questions. They are mainly about Agni. I don't feel afraid or anything like that. I have this burning sensation that Agni knows things about my life that I don't. Things that I probably would know if I hadn't lost my memory. Then there's this anger about not knowing and realizing that what I can't remember could put people in danger. Not knowing also makes me feel guilty. I had a family who loved me that I can't even remember. I don't talk about how much the amnesia bothers me. But I have times when it gets under my skin. And Agni isn't helping."

"I can't say that I can help with that. I can't even say that I understand. Just know that the Flamethrowers want to help, and we won't leave you when you need us most. We aren't afraid either," Arrow sighed.

"I know." Jai walked away from the window and sat on his bed. Arrow was already starting to drift off to sleep; however, Jai wasn't tired. The pulsing energy from the volcano was keeping him awake. He couldn't shake the feeling that something was slightly off. Carefully, he headed to the door and proceeded to go outside to the back of the palace near the volcano.

Jai intended to see the volcano, but he stopped when he noticed Arin sitting on her knees on the stone slab. There was a gentle evening breeze that captured strands of her short black hair and made them dance in the direction of the wind. The rise and fall of her shoulders was rhythmic, she seemed so calm and peaceful. But it pained Jai to see her alone. He noticed her body tremble a bit as if she suddenly became cold. Instinctively he touched his arms, but his upper body was only clothed by a vest. He had no coat to offer her. How could someone radiate that much beauty when you aren't even looking at their face? Jai quietly walked toward her, hoping his presence would offer her pleasant company.

"You okay, Arin?"

"Yeah," she didn't even look in his direction.

Feeling like *yeah* meant *no*, Jai decided to talk to her instead. He slowly sat on his knees beside her. The sun had set hours ago, and it was dark. The moon was almost full, its light gently illuminating her face, enhancing her natural beauty.

"What's wrong?"

"Nothing," she replied sharply, never making eye contact with him.

Jai sighed and stretched his legs out before laying down on the slab, "Is this how you normally are? Was that happy person just you being nice?"

"What?" she looked at him, puzzled by his question.

"There's nothing wrong with it. Duty can change people, and sometimes once you're away from it, all you want is peace and quiet."

"No, I just have things on my mind right now," she whispered before looking back toward the edge of Pyroc.

Leaning close to her, Jai spoke softly, "I was just asking. Everyone has been making accommodations for me, and I know that I'm doing nothing for them. It feels strange. Back in Ember, Arka gave me a lot, but he also expected a lot from me. I guess I'm saying that it feels like everyone, especially the Flamethrowers, is giving me so much and I'm just taking and not giving anything back. That's why I'm trying to get to know everyone and respect everything I'm being given."

Her light brown eyes looked up toward him, "You're giving us a lot too. This People's War has lasted for almost three hundred years. People are tired and are giving up on the Universe and themselves. They are broken and divided, with no one strong enough to turn things around. Your very existence gives the world hope. And for the Firehearts, you're our sign of freedom. That in itself means a lot," Arin replied.

"I like talking to you. I feel like we have complimentary energy. I just wanted to try and understand what you were feeling. I've never seen you just sitting alone. My intention wasn't to pry."

"I appreciate that. Sorry, I was rude earlier. My thoughts were just somewhere else."

"Somewhere like?"

"Have you ever wanted to be someone else?" she asked.

"Yeah, I guess after meeting Aqila, I want to be like her. Fire is about freedom. She had freedom and knew her destiny and was chasing it feverishly. It motivated me. I love how the Flamethrowers made a conscious choice to be Flamethrowers. Still, it's different when the Universe decides who you will be. The Universe decided that Aqila would be a seer. She never once hid that she was one. I always had to hide my gift, fearing it would change the color of my eyes and anger Arka, and I'd be abandoned with nowhere to call home. Then after Aqila told me about the previous Legends, I knew why the Universe sent her my way."

"Why?" She averted her gaze.

"To tell me to be myself, embrace everything that I am. And also, as a Legend, to embrace everything that I'm not. I needed someone to tell me that," Jai sighed.

Arin giggled softly, "In that case, I'm glad you met her too. I just want to see you realize your destiny and find your purpose. I'm in your corner, and I believe in you. I know about your amnesia. I can't imagine how hard all of this change must be. But I'm here for you."

Jai chuckled, "Yeah, I've known that from the start. I've never said this, but I appreciate it."

"Anytime," she whispered and gently patted his shoulder. "I'm going to sleep, Jai. Thanks for coming to talk to me." She stood to leave.

Jai didn't move. "Anytime," he replied. Arin went back inside the palace. Jai sighed, feeling relieved that everything was okay with her. Slowly, he sat up and stared at the volcano. He could still feel her presence lingering beside him. It was so comforting. In the distance, he heard voices. As Jai quietly approached the volcano, he saw Cahya and Calida. They seemed to be in a heated argument.

"I can't believe you're not coming with me! She's our mother," Cahya fumed.

"I can't just leave the Flamethrowers! I'm their leader. I have to protect them," Calida retorted.

"I'm going with or without you!"

"Cahya, listen to me—"

"No! You listen! Father named you the leader of the Flamethrowers. That's fine. I have always supported your decisions, good or bad. But when he died, he made me the man of the house. It's my job to put my life on the line for your and mother's safety. Bottomline! When are you going to support me in my duty?"

"I can't leave them," Calida firmly replied.

"Fine, then don't," Cahya began to walk away. "It's simple. You won't find me here in the morning."

"Cahya, stop!"

"Leave me alone," Cahya bellowed and threw a fire-laced punch at his sister.

Calida narrowly ducked, "Why would you do that?" she yelled, then fire punched at him.

The pair engaged in a heated battle. Calida kicked and punched fire at her younger brother. Cahya never seemed phased and expertly dodged her attacks, violently countering with his own. To Jai's surprise, Calida was a good fighter, but Cahya easily outmatched her. His personality was a complete contrast to his abilities as a Fireheart. Cahya pushed his sister away, and she lost her balance, hitting the ground hard.

Cahya turned to walk away. "As I said, I'm leaving."

Calida grabbed her bow and arrow, and Cahya shook his head as he readied his bow. He turned, and at that moment, they both released an arrow. "Ignite!" Cahya bellowed.

Both arrowheads made violent contact, and immediately, two flaming creatures erupted. They appeared as phoenixes, with Cahya's noticeably larger than Calida's. The phoenixes fought intensely.

In a vast, open sky, the two clashed, their feathers ablaze with orange and red flames and flecks of blue embers. They circled each other, their eyes locked onto their opponent. Cahya's phoenix was larger, with feathers that blazed brighter than the sun. It dove toward its opponent, its sharp talons poised to strike. Calida's phoenix was smaller but no less fierce, with a wingspan that seemed to stretch for miles. It met its opponent head-on, its own talons clashing with Cahya's phoenix.

As they tangled in mid-air, their fiery feathers ruffled and sparked. The larger phoenix managed to gain the upper hand, pinning its opponent to the ground with a fierce claw strike. But the smaller phoenix was not so easily defeated. It broke free, its feathers sparking as it launched a counterattack. The two winged creatures continued to fight, their movements swift and fluid as they soared through the sky. Flames licked at their feathers, creating an intense, radiating heat. They dove and swooped, their beaks clashing as they fought for dominance.

In this battle of wills, Calida's phoenix began to weaken, its movements becoming slower and less precise. Jai stood in awe, having never seen anything of such magnitude before. Cahya's phoenix consumed Calida's, leaving nothing but a pile of ash in its place.

"I don't even know why you tried that. Enough, Cal, we aren't children anymore. I'm leaving. At least one of us cares enough about Mom to help her when she needs us." Cahya took a deep breath and resumed his usual demeanor. Calida lay on the ground, defeated by her younger brother. With nothing but his bow and quiver filled with arrows, Cahya continued walking past the volcano as if nothing had ever happened.

Jai hurried to Calida's side. She was sweating, and stray hairs were falling around her forehead. Her eyes widened upon seeing him. "How much did you see?"

"I heard some noises and came this way. I just saw you laying here and that shadow walking away," Jai lied. "Are you okay?"

"I'm fine. That was Cahya; we argued and roughed each other up a bit."

"What's going on?"

She sighed a long, heavy sigh. Finally sitting up, she replied, "Our mother sent a message to the cabin, and it was forwarded to us. Agni captured her. He wants her to reveal where the Flamethrowers have taken the Legend. She wouldn't speak, so he will probably try to burn the entire forest to force us out. He already knows that's where we hide out; he just has not had a hunter good enough to travel that far. But, if he burns it down, he won't need one."

"What are you going to do?"

"I have to protect the Flamethrowers. My father left me in charge of his legacy." She touched the golden ring on her chain. "I have to protect them. Cahya wants to break Mother out of Agni's headquarters, and he can try. Our mom is a Flamethrower as well. She would never give us away. I want to help, but I have to protect the family legacy. I hate that Cahya is acting like I don't love Mom, or he loves her more than I do!"

"You're willing to let your mother suffer and possibly die?"

"I don't want her to die, but I can't jeopardize the mission. I made a promise to my father. You're here. The Legend is here. I'm going to fight for this," Calida replied.

"Cahya is not wrong for wanting to save her. Why can't you send a message? Everyone can leave safely and you can help your brother."

"It's not just the people! The cabin, the history, the rules, maps, everything! They've been in our family for hundreds of years. Generations of my family have held this sacred duty! I have to protect that part of our history. It was entrusted to me!"

"There has to be a way to do both. But you can't narrow your sight on one part of the problem," Jai reflected.

Calida stood up and pointed at Jai. "Look, we have two different realities. You're in no position to judge me! What do you know about family? You can't even remember yours!" She paused, "Jai—I'm sorry. I should not have said that."

Jai slowly stood up, "I'm not judging you, Calida. You want to move the Flamethrowers from the forest. I get that, but you can do that from here. Like you've done everything else—messenger hawk, signals, and whatever. You're not wrong for wanting to save them, but you're running too. You want to return to the forest and fight to protect everything your family has built. I understand that. It's honorable. But your mother is a Flamethrower too, and she might need you right now.

"The Flamethrowers can build a new home, but can you find a new mother? Your mother is also a part of your father's legacy. No, I don't know much about family, but don't you start to forget what you know! We are Firehearts. We are courageous. Our passion for what we believe in gives us strength and power. That doesn't mean that we don't have fears. It just means we don't let fear stand between us and victory. I'm not going to stand here and be a reason why you don't fight for your family. Your family always fought for you. Bring the Flamethrowers here, and we can break your mother out together."

Calida sighed, "That cabin and those hideouts have been there for almost three hundred years. So many memories of my father and grandfather are within those walls, and I can't imagine not fighting for them. My father died for me. We went to Ember a few years ago and Agni's soldiers were there looking for people to join their cause. My father, Dehateh, stood up to them. He openly challenged their ideas of hunting a Legend. A fight broke out, and he hurried to take me back to the forest for my safety. Agni's soldiers threw a fire dagger at my face. I fell, and the soldier was ready to strike me dead with a flaming sword—" she stopped.

Jai hung his head, knowing what she was about to say.

She sobbed, "Dad ran in front of me and was struck instead."

Jai grabbed Calida and enveloped him in his arms.

"I ran to the forest to get Mom. He was already dead when Mom arrived at the scene. He entrusted everything he had to me. He trusted me. He died for me. If he was still here, Agni wouldn't have Mom."

"Calida, the forest is important, but so is your mother. I can't imagine what it's like to hold everything together after having watched your father be murdered in front of you. If we can work together so your mother doesn't have that same fate, let's do that. We can do this."

She pulled away from him and wiped her eyes. Her back was straight and tall, eyes confident as she said, "I'll bring the Flamethrowers here immediately, then we can join Cahya. I'll tell Arrow everything in the morning."

"If there is anything I can do to help, I'll do it."

"Thanks," Calida replied. "Well, I'm going to prepare a message for the hawk. Good night."

Jai waved and started back toward the palace. Calida watched him leave and smiled to herself while touching the ring. "Dad, the Legend is better than we could have ever hoped. He's like a gentle fire that brings light and warmth. We'll try our best to support him, just like you taught me. I pray to the Stars that we can keep him alive."

CHAPTER 12

A part of Jai was drained; the other part of him was screaming with questions—burning questions that threatened to singe his brain. Jai returned to the room he shared now only with Arrow, who was sleeping peacefully. Although Jai wanted to rest, he couldn't. He felt responsible for what happened to Cahya and Calida's parents. Jai tried to think back as far as he could. Had he ever met Agni? He couldn't recall. That name sounded entirely unfamiliar to him. What could he possibly want from him? Did it have something to do with Arka? There was this wrenching feeling inside him that knew whatever Agni wanted, Jai wouldn't be able to give him and continue to live. Then it came to him: Zay!

Zay followed Arrow and Jai to the forest, and before he left, he said he'd have to report it to Agni. That's how Agni must have found out. He must have already known about the Flamethrowers' presence but could never find the precise location until now. Jai felt guilty. Agni found the cabin because of him. He was more determined than ever to confront Agni and find out his intentions once and for all.

"What's wrong?"

"I thought you were asleep," Jai said.

"I was, but I—I felt something off." Arrow sat up; his amber eyes had a subtle glow against the deep hues of the night.

"How do you know all of this stuff about Legends?"

Arrow chuckled, "Growing up here, you have to be well informed about a lot of things. I'm a Dragon Prince. If anything were to happen to Sheraga, I would be next in line to be DragonLord. Once I started learning about history and the different people, I could not stop."

"So Sheraga knows a lot about Legends too?"

"Sheraga knows what Sheraga knows," he chuckled. "But yes, contrary to popular belief, my brother is well educated. My parents requested teachers from every nation and territory, except the Waterbearers, to come and teach us."

"That's unbelievable!"

"Well, we are rulers; education is important. Is there something you wanted to know?"

"Yes. If Cyra was such a horrible Legend, why are the Flamethrowers so dedicated to her? If she was so bad, why would anyone want to help me?"

"History is a funny thing. Sometimes, it is only one side of a multi-dimensional truth. Cyra didn't leave a written text like Basir did. Everything we know about her is directly from the stories passed down from generations, and the sages' recordings fill in the rest. Did she do some awful things? Yes. Was that her whole story? Absolutely not! Cyra made a mistake, and that mistake had consequences. But she learned from it. She changed and tried to make things right. In the end, Cyra sacrificed her life to atone for what she could not fix. She was a Legend, a warrior, even a general, but she was also human."

"So there's more than just starting a family with a Waterbearer, getting him murdered, and starting a war?"

"Yes, a whole lot more. Cyra saved my great-great-grandmother after she was kidnapped by

Emberites as a baby. She appeared giftless for most of her life, yet rose through the ranks of DragonGuard to become a general. She was shunned by her family as a teenager. She had been heartbroken several times before she met Aenon. She made him realize his greater destiny. She worked to ensure equality throughout the Fireheart territories. She was a warrior against injustice. After the death of her daughter, she started Flamethrower lodges to help children who'd lost their parents to war and teach them what she knew best: survival skills. Cyra raised these orphans as her own children. She even found her soulmate. Now, has anyone ever told you about any of that?"

"Not at all!"

"My mother used to say that everyone's life is parallel to a war. There are victories and losses. The final verdict is made at death. If you win the war, your spirit will ascend to the Stars and take its place among every other champion that has ever lived. If you lose, your spirit dies and is laid to rest with your body."

A warm feeling washed over Jai as he listened to Arrow speak of his mother. "What was she like?"

"Who? My mother?"

Jai nodded.

Arrow lowered his head, "She was the best mother anyone could ask for. I just wish I took the time to tell her that."

"If she ascended to the Stars, she already knows."

"I guess you're right."

A brief moment of silence came between them. "Arrow, what is this team? I've heard it mentioned a few times."

"Well, they call themselves different things: squad, band, alliance, and so on. But it's just the other Legends. There are only two specific roles: the Golden-Eyed Legend and the One Who Knows."

"The One Who Knows?"

"Yeah, so the order of the Legends mirrors the order of the Universe: Fire, Wind, Water, and Land. Fireheart Legend is always first, and the nationality of the One Who Knows alternates between the rest; I don't know the order. The One Who Knows realizes they are a Legend very early in life, and they usually go on a journey to find other Legends like themselves."

"It can't be that hard! I mean, once everyone knows that they are a Legend, aren't other people willing to help?"

"Oh no! It doesn't work like that. The One Who Knows can't reveal their identity to the other Legends, and they tend not to reveal this information to anyone. I don't know why that happens. I'm not a Legend. Firehearts are never the One Who Knows, so I can't explain that part of it that well."

"I'm relieved. I'm glad Cyra was able to redeem herself, even if it was just a little bit."

"Same. Life isn't easy. I know I'm a Dragon Prince, and I've grown up in a luxury that most people can't even imagine, but everyone faces hardship. Following the Universal Order is not always easy. But it must be done. I mean, I've never been attracted to any other nationality other than my own, but wonderful people exist outside of Firehearts. But if we are to ascend to the Stars, we must be strong and stay true to the Order."

"Now it makes sense! Everyone seemed a little tense the second I said Aqila was pretty," Jai laughed.

"I know! At least she's engaged, so that won't be an issue," Arrow chuckled.

Jai stretched out on the bed, "How does it feel to be home?"

"You can't imagine how good it feels. I ran away nearly four years ago. I'm thankful for the journey. I would not have met Calida or become a Flamethrower if I hadn't. I would not have met you if I hadn't left. I missed out on important things here; my brother got married and was crowned. My mother passed and I did not even show up for her burial. However, I am finally making some victories. I finally can feel my dragon energy again. It's vivid and alive. I didn't realize exactly what I gave up until I didn't have it."

"Now you have it back."

"Not everything. I ran away from home and dishonored my family. Forgiveness from the people will take a while. But I understand. Crazy thing is, I nearly started a battle on the edge of Pyroc and Lower Ember when I was younger. I was showing off to my fellow soldiers, trying to outdo Sheraga . . . attempting to, at least. We were new DragonGuards. At that age, we weren't allowed at the border without senior DragonGuards with us. As usual, I was breaking the rules. We were young and irresponsible. I led my group over the borderline, and we were practicing with our dragon energy. We accidentally burned part of the forest."

"I panicked, and Yuuna tried to contain the fire with no luck. See, dragon energy has its drawbacks; we all experience the struggle to contain flames, especially at the ages we were at that time. So basically, we made everything worse. Some Emberites confronted us, and they were angry; of course, we were destroying their territory. Sheraga was doing a military exercise not far away. He comes, though, because of the smoke; everyone is yelling and mad, and Sheraga was trying to de-escalate. Then someone attacked me, and I killed him. Sheraga went the hell off because someone attacked me. The Emberites began attacking Sheraga. I ran away, leaving him and my friends behind. That worsened tensions between Pyroc and Lower Ember. My brother ended up killing a few Emberites to protect the inexperienced DragonGuard, and Lower Ember wanted to hang him for war crimes. It got pretty bad. My parents nearly disowned me after that."

"Damn!"

"Yeah, I know. I lost the respect of the DragonGuard after that. Yuuna got put out of the Guard because of it. Her parents did disown her. I felt so bad, Yuuna doesn't have the strongest dragon energy; she doesn't even have the pulse scales. But she was trying so hard. I messed up really bad. The only reason I was tolerated was that, Holy Stars, everyone knows better than to piss Sheraga off. That is like a death sentence."

"Poor Yuuna. Her parents disowned her? That's horrible."

"Yeah, I felt horrible. It's one of the big reasons Pyre hates me. He was absolutely in love with Yuuna. His family would not allow him to marry her anymore."

"That's crazy!"

"Status is kinda the thing around here. Family status is important, with military honors earning some of the highest status."

"Do you plan on coming back to this? I mean, it seems like you enjoy being a Flamethrower."

"I do. I feel like at some point I am going to return to fulfilling my duty as Dragon Prince. The pressure won't really be on me to do that until my brother starts having children. Then my father will be pushing me to marry and fulfill my obligations."

Jai sighed, and silence fell upon them. Growing up in Pyroc seemed equally as complicated as growing up in Lower Ember.

"You know something I noticed? Pyroc doesn't have giftless Firehearts," Jai spoke.

Arrow burst into laughter, "Since when?"

"I haven't seen any so far."

"Yeah, and this is the palace, home of the dragons! The most powerful dragons are situated right here. Of course you don't run into giftless people in these parts. Jai, being giftless can come from a lot of things. It's not necessarily bad. Think of it as a recessive trait."

"In Lower Ember, most of the population is giftless. Some lost their gifts, like Arka. But others, like Zay, just never had one. Most who had a gift left for Upper Ember once they reached adulthood. In Lower Ember, you get exiled for being gifted."

"Ember has a unique history with people and gifts, but most times not having a gift has more to do with how the heavenly bodies were aligned at birth. Now, Aqila is an expert on this topic. She studied astronomy and how it correlates to spirituality or something. What I'm saying is, she can explain it better. My best understanding is that certain gifts are manifested through how the Sun, Moon, and other planets were aligned at the time of your birth. Fire, Wind, Water, and Land abilities require specific

Sun-Moon alignment at the time of birth. If that is not present, then one is born giftless. Being giftless results in dark-brown eyes because the power of one's gift is what produces eye color."

"So, two giftless people could have a child who is gifted?"

"Under that circumstance, yes. There is also the case of being born under a curse, like Cyra and Aenon's twin girls. That would produce dark-brown eyes also. And people who completely disbelieve in the Universe after already having a gift can lose it. Such was probably the case with Arka. Even though that happens, it is not as common as the misalignment of the Sun and Moon."

"I never knew that."

Arrow yawned and lowered himself on his bed until he was lying flat. "Well, now you know."

Finally, Jai was completely exhausted. His brain felt like it was moments from shutting down from the overload of information. He lay down, his eyelids feeling as if they were carrying the weight of the world. He wondered about a lot of things—Arka, Agni, and his family. Could Agni have something to do with the family he couldn't remember? The radiating heat from the volcano in the distance was the only blanket of comfort Jai had. It was nice to have friends, however. In the quiet of night, all the thoughts and feelings he'd pushed away came crashing down upon him. Jai squeezed his eyes shut, as he could no longer resist the urge to sleep.

CHAPTER 13

The following day, Jai woke up and realized that he was late. He hopped out of bed, bolted downstairs, and dashed to the back of the palace. Sheraga was calmly sitting on his knees. "I didn't think you were coming," he said flatly.

"I'm sorry for being late," Jai puffed, catching his breath.

"Relax; I'm in a talking mood today, lucky for you. Sit," he tilted his head toward the space to his right. "What do you know about the First People?"

"The what?"

"I guess that means you know nothing about them. The history of the First People is very important to the

Firehearts. I strongly believe that no Fireheart, regardless of their ability or background, should be void of this knowledge. I don't know anything about the plight of a Legend. But I do know that the Fireheart Legend is always born first and sets the tone for what the Legends as a group will accomplish. It oddly corresponds with our place as the First People."

Sheraga continued, "As our history tells it, the first men were born from a raging fire. They were a trio who wielded powers likened to the fire which they came from. Later on, three men were born from the wind. Then three women were born from a river, and last, three people, two men and one woman, were born from dust and dirt. Finally, on the last day of year one, twelve stars fell from the sky. Each star transformed into either a man or a woman. They came with twenty revelations that comprise what we call today the Universal Order. After the revelation, their eyes turned to the deepest shade of brown and they intermingled with the First People. If that didn't happen, there would not be any Firehearts, Windmasters, Waterbearers, or Landkeepers as we know them today."

"The first men were Firehearts and the first Legend in a cycle is always a Fireheart. The sun was the first creation in the Universe, and we are the people of the Sun. Education is a very important part of my upbringing. As Firehearts, I feel it is important to know where we came from."

"Thank you, Sheraga."

Jai was sitting on his knees. Sheraga nodded his head, "I'm going to be very honest with you. For what you said you wanted, you no longer need me."

Jai's jaw dropped, "What do you mean?"

"You said you wanted to learn fire, and you have. It's as simple as that. You didn't say that you wanted to be a soldier, make volcanoes explode, or breathe fire. You just said you wanted to learn how to use it, and you have."

"So that's it? One overly strenuous day of exercise is all I get?"

Sheraga laughed, "It wasn't my idea, but my father advised me regarding you. He emphasized the importance of you discovering the depths of your own gift. As one matures, sometimes their gifts evolve into supplemental abilities. He also said that not taking the time to discover the beauty in the Universe's gift was the beginning of the downfall of Cyra."

"Aqila was telling me the same thing yesterday," Jai murmured.

"I'm not saying I won't help you. I will be your ally. But I can't train you like a soldier because you're a Legend. You have to show me what you need, for you have a gift unlike any other. Come on." Sheraga stood, his red robe barely brushing the stone slab. He walked to the opposite side of the slab and tossed his robe aside, revealing his naturally muscular form. His well-defined abdominal muscles were laced with the outline of greenish dragon scales. And his back had a large tattoo of a dragon spewing fire from its mouth. Jai got into a fighting stance, mirroring Sheraga. He focused on his gift and took several deep breaths.

"I thought I was done training?"

"We never got a good spar on," Sheraga laughed. He shot a massive fire punch his way. Jai met the fire with a light-balling punch. Upon contact, they both dissipated.

"Good," Sheraga called, "you know now that a light ball and a fireball will cancel each other out. Let's keep going." Sheraga displayed a combination front kick followed by a roundhouse kick. Jai met the attack with an aggressive punch and side-kick combination. His attack started with light that turned to fire as the strikes neared Sheraga's body. Sheraga moved the fire easily, "All right, you can turn the light into fire."

"Yeah, thanks to you," Jai replied.

"Try turning the fire into light," Sheraga instructed.

Jai charged Sheraga in a fiery punching attack. Sheraga was a master and could quickly turn the flames to his advantage, allowing his offense to also serve as his defense. While Sheraga and Jai sparred, Jai intentionally allowed some sparks to fall on the ground. When Sheraga's sheer strength and power became too challenging to handle, Jai dropped back. With a sweeping motion, he made a wall of fire between himself and Sheraga. When Sheraga went to manipulate the firewall himself and create an advantage, Jai took a deep breath and turned the fire into a wall of light. Sheraga groaned and turned away momentarily. With his eyes closed, he moved around the wall and punched an intense fire in Jai's direction, knocking him to the ground. The light dissipated, and Sheraga stopped. He extended a hand to help Jai up. Jai accepted and began to pull up. Sheraga pushed him back down violently.

"Come on, man!"

"I don't care what battle you're in: don't make a habit of accepting your opponent's hand of grace. It could be a trap, and I'd hate for you to learn that the hard way." Sheraga backed up, giving Jai room to get up. "I think you're good to go. You can turn light into fire and fire into light. For what you asked of me, my job is done."

"Yeah, you still got me in the end." Jai stood up.

"True, but I'm experienced in battle in addition to being born into the DragonLord family. You did well. Just keep practicing." Sheraga put his robe on before turning to leave. Jai's skin was sticky with sweat. Sheraga looked completely refreshed as if the exercise was a mere stretching routine.

He was going easy on me. I'd hate to meet him on a battlefield.

"Thank you," Jai called out to him. Sheraga humbly nodded and continued back inside the palace. Jai noticed Arin and Alena peeking around the side of the palace.

"You know I can see you two, right?"

"Wow, Jai! You did so well," Arin cheered for him.

"Exactly! That was some technique you've got. You could probably pull light straight from the sun!" Alena chimed in.

"I don't know about all of that." Jai scratched his head at their enthusiasm. "Where's Calida and Arrow?"

"They're having a discussion. Cahya left all of a sudden. We wanted to join in, but they shooed us away," Arin sighed.

"I don't know what's going on, but let's go to town and do something while we have some time for ourselves," Alena suggested.

"And do what?"

Alena thought about Jai's question, "Get candy crystals! I bet Aqila didn't take you there!" Alena mockingly rolled Aqila's name from her tongue before running off. Arin lowered her head and followed her twin. Unsure of why his friendship with the apprentice seer was a big deal, he shrugged his shoulders. As he followed in the direction of Alena and Arin, he hoped that the talk between Calida and Arrow would go all right. The walk about town went quickly; the candy crystal shop was not too far away.

"It's this one," Alena exclaimed. The quaint shop sat nestled in the heart of the bustling military town. The small storefront was adorned with a vintage wooden sign hanging overhead that read "Sweet Delights." The sisters peered into the glass window. When Jai looked, he saw candies of different colors on a wooden stick.

"Which one is flaming cherry?" Jai asked Arin.

"The darkest red one," she said, pointing to one in the display case.

"I think I want to try that one."

"Hey, you have to try the hot chocolate one too," Alena complained. She entered the shop, and Arin and Jai stayed outside.

"You don't want to go inside?"

"Nah. My sister will just about buy the whole store. No point going in," Arin chuckled. She looked at Jai from the corner of her eye, "Do you like it in Pyroc?"

"Yes, it's nice here, but I miss being in Ember," Jai admitted to her.

"Really? You miss being in Lower Ember?" Arin was shocked at his response.

"Yeah, I miss the people. Yes, there were hard times. It's nothing like the shops and events here, but the people are more interconnected. People with very little trying to help those who had nothing. I miss that feeling and want to help Lower Ember be a better place with more opportunities. Still, I don't want those last threads of community to be lost," Jai explained.

"I understand," Arin murmured.

Suddenly, Alena tapped on the window to get the pair's attention. She wanted them to join her. Once inside, the atmosphere changed entirely. The buzzing of the street faded away, replaced by the sound of soft music playing in the background. The air was filled with the sweet aroma of sugar and chocolate, enveloping them as they stepped through the door. The walls were lined with shelves packed full of candy jars and boxes of various sizes and shapes. Gummy bears, sour worms, and licorice sticks sat alongside chocolate bars, fudge, and homemade toffee. Old-fashioned lollipops and taffy sticks were displayed in a glass case at the counter.

The shopkeeper, a friendly woman with a beaming smile, stood behind the counter ready to assist customers in selecting their treats. Her hair was styled in a neat blood-red bun, and she wore a basic blush pink short-sleeved dress, adding to the charm of the store.

In the back of the store, a small seating area with wooden tables and chairs offered a cozy spot for customers to enjoy their treats. While Jai was observing the shop, Alena was getting a paper bag filled with candies.

As they stepped back out into the street, Arin asked, "What did you get?"

Alena wiggled her eyebrows, "A little bit of everything!" She reached into the bag while walking toward them. She pulled out handfuls of candy and stuffed them into Arin and Jai's pockets until they were full. "Treats are on me!"

"Thanks," Jai and Arin said in unison.

The trio began to make their way back to the palace.

"I hope everything's going well with Calida and Arrow," Alena said, her words somewhat choppy with the candy crystal in her mouth.

"Yeah, it's been on my mind all morning," Arin replied.

"Cahya is my best friend. I just can't believe he left like that, especially without saying anything," Alena sighed.

"I know. That's not like him at all," Arin agreed.

"Well, it must have been something important." Jai shrugged his shoulders. Arin tilted her head toward him after he spoke. The look in her eyes was questioning. Then she looked away. Jai hoped that she did not think he knew more than they did.

I'm glad she didn't press the issue about it.

When they returned, Sheraga and Liora were in battle armor. They stood tall in their dragon-style golden armor, the intricate designs on their breastplates gleaming in the bright sun. Their helmets were shaped like dragon heads, with sharp teeth and red eyes that seemed to glow with intensity. The couple both carried long, curved swords at their sides, their blades glinting in the light. Liora's sword had a hilt adorned with rubies, while Sheraga's had a handle wrapped in black leather. They both wore black boots that came up to their knees, and their gauntlets were studded with diamonds.

Calida and Arrow seemed to be in a semi-heated conversation off to the left of the DragonLord and DragonLady.

"I hope we're not walking into an active volcano. Those two look like they are ready for battle," Alena murmured, quickly finishing her candy. They hurried past the palace soldiers, who never broke their formation. The twins went to Calida and Arrow, but Jai stopped at the DragonLord.

"Don't worry, I'm not going to war," Sheraga started, seeing the puzzled expression on Jai's face. "Liora and I just finished some drills with the DragonGuard. I have some urgent business in Kindle that I must see to. I may be gone for a week or two. Until I return, my wife will be acting in my stead. Jai, I may not see you for a while, especially if the Flamethrowers are leaving, but I wish you the best in all your endeavors."

"Thank you for all your help. I hope we cross paths soon." Jai shook the DragonLord's hand. He headed toward the Flamethrowers, and everyone stopped talking when he came close. "I hate it when you all do that," Jai groaned.

"Sorry, Jai, we are just trying to work out some details," Arrow acknowledged.

"Cahya didn't say where he was going to start looking for Mom," Calida groaned.

"Well, it has to be on the border of Upper and Lower Ember. That's where Arrow said Aqila had the vision of the headquarters. An apprentice seer is still a seer. That would probably be where Cahya started looking," Alena reminded.

"Well, that's a start," Calida sighed. "The rest of the Flamethrowers are meeting us here by the afternoon. Then we are going to head to the border and spread out to look for Cahya or anything that resembles a headquarters. Jai, you're going to need this," she handed him a black hood. The material was lightweight but would work well in covering his face.

"Thanks, Calida," he replied, accepting the hood.

"Don't mention it. It was Arin's idea," Calida patted Arin on the shoulder.

"This actually ended up being good timing. My brother is going to meet with Tora; if we run into any major issues, he won't be far away," Arrow reflected.

"That's true, but we want to keep Pyroc out of this as much as possible. We don't want to tip the scale in favor of a civil war between the Firehearts. We can't forget that Lower Ember supports Agni's views," Calida reminded.

"Yeah, then we'd look like Theyra: Landkeeper versus Landkeeper," Arin chimed in. Hearing that Theyra was in a civil war made Jai feel uneasy. Aqila was headed there, and he hoped that she would be careful. Did she know what she was getting herself into? In the distance, he could see the rest of the Flamethrowers from the forest approaching them.

"Arrow," Sheraga called, "I'll be gone for a couple of weeks. You know where to find me. Take care, brother." They shook hands before Sheraga mounted his Komodo dragon, Ash. His armor gleamed in the light. He sat astride Ash with ease, one hand firmly gripping the reins while the other rested on the hilt of his sword. The massive creature beneath him moved with graceful and fearsome power, its scales rippling with each stride. The Komodo dragon let out a low growl, its forked tongue flicking in and out as it sniffed the air. It darted off with its rider. Liora watched her husband leave before returning to the palace. Jai wondered about Liora. Sheraga trusted her with everything that belonged to him. She must be a reliable woman.

"Hey, team!" Suvan shouted as they got closer.

"How's everything been?" Arrow asked him.

"Everything was going pretty well, no issues at all, except for those letters," Suvan replied.

"We did one last check, and we didn't see any pending attacks set for the forest. Quiver did her best to consolidate your family's belongings and secure them before we left. It was short notice, but she gave it her best," Dysis chimed.

"I moved everything to the Westward forest. If Agni destroys our current location, the cabin in Westward will be our next secure location. I hope you are okay with that, Calida," Quiver spoke.

"That's good, thank you. We are going to the border of Upper and Lower Ember to find Agni's headquarters. He has my mother captive, and Cahya has gone to free her. We will help him as best we can while attacking Agni.

We aren't sure what kind of forces he has, but he must be compact anytime he can stay hidden so well," Calida explained.

"Or he could be hiding in plain sight. With the complete support of Lower Ember, there's no reason to hide," Quiver commented.

"Either way, it's horrible. I hope Cahya is doing okay," Dysis murmured.

A hazel-eyed young man asked, "Have we been divided into groups yet? We can't all go searching on the border without drawing suspicion."

"Yes, Kiran, we have made groups," Arrow answered. "Group One is to be Cahya's backup. This group includes Calida, Yuuna, and Beamer; the mission is to help Cahya free Sitara. Group Two is to infiltrate Agni's headquarters. This includes Arin, Alena, Kiran, and Flame. Their mission is to allow for the entrance and exit of Group Three. The third group is to corner Agni. Group Three includes Jai, Suvan, and me. Dysis and Quiver will go back to complete the preparation of our new base location in the Westward forest," Arrow instructed.

"You asked for all of us to come only to send some of us back?" Dysis was not thrilled over the news as she placed her hands on her hips.

"Arrow and I want to preserve all the history of the Flamethrowers that we can. I know you said Quiver started, but if we can get everything, that would be most helpful."

"What about Cahya?" Dysis pressed.

"It'll be fine, Dysis. He is getting backup," Yuuna replied in hopes of calming her friend.

The fair-skinned, honey-eyed girl known as Quiver spoke, "Should we meet you once we are done?"

"There's no need for that. Our emergency exit plan is to take the shortest route to Kindle. The location is near the Theyra-Kindle border, where the hot dunes are. We'll take refuge there if the worst happens," Calida instructed. The Flamethrowers began to disperse. Quiver was preparing to leave with Dysis, who was staring off into space. Her usual confidence was worn away with worry.

Jai walked over to her. "Everything will be okay, Dysis."

She sighed. "I just wish I was there to have Cahya's back." She dropped her head. "We've always had each other's back."

"You have his back. You'll be protecting his family legacy. He'll understand."

Dysis nodded before rejoining Quiver. They departed for their part of the operation. Jai watched until the pair was no longer in sight. He was hopeful for the success of all the groups. Moments later, the first group departed, led by Calida. Arrow explained that the second and third groups would be leaving together. Jai could tell that most were nervous. He just prayed to the Universe that the success of this mission would get Agni off their tails for a while. Jai noticed how young most of the Flamethrowers were. Arrow, Calida, and Yuuna were older than him by a couple of years. Suvan was around his age. However, the rest of them were two or more years younger. Quiver, Beamer, and Flame were barely teenagers. He didn't like the idea of Beamer and Flame joining them. They were probably better off going with Dysis and Quiver to Westward.

Arrow and Calida are more experienced; they probably know what's best.

Jai was trying hard to settle his thoughts until he felt someone bump his shoulder.

"So, how was training with the mighty DragonLord?" Suvan asked, failing horribly at whispering.

"It was, like you said, very intense. I really did think that I was going to fall out, but I didn't. Sheraga just drilled me and drilled me until I gave him a perfect set," Jai explained.

"Which gets harder to do the more tired you are," Suvan added.

"Exactly. Afterward, I thought I was getting a break, and the man wanted to spar!" The pair laughed.

"Seems like you got it easy, and he wasn't training you to be a soldier. So you got lucky," Suvan shared.

"I didn't know you trained for the military." Jai raised his eyebrows.

"Yeah, I trained here to qualify for the Upper Ember Military. I got in easily, but I didn't like the atmosphere. It wasn't horrible or anything. I just didn't fit in. The dragon energy thing doesn't sit well with me. It gets me unsettled and ruins my performance. So I left the military after a year and joined the Flame Eaters. They are an incredible acrobatic group. I did that for another year, and then I started performing hypnosis in a traveling circus. That lasted until I got recruited for the Flamethrowers. Now, it's like the best of both worlds. I can use my military training and my gift to full capacity."

Jai would have never guessed that Suvan had performed as a Flame Eater or was in a traveling circus. He added, "I also got a chance to do a little sightseeing. And I met Aqila, the apprentice seer."

"Whoa, you lucked up! She's really nice, but don't get on her bad side. She's a Storm and will turn the place upside down. When she puts her foot down, the sky comes down too."

"Yeah, I've heard that. But I liked that about her," Jai smiled.

"Speaking of the silver-eyed giant, did she have a vision for you?"

"No, but she gave me her word that if she did, she'd let me know."

"All right, take your positions. We're leaving now," Arrow commanded everyone's attention. Everyone went to their respective groups and began for the Pyrocean border. Liora and the DragonGuard waved them off with a salute. Every step they took led Jai farther from the constant calling of the volcanoes. He understood why Pyroc was quite the attraction for Firehearts of all backgrounds. He promised himself that he would come back and visit. For now, he focused on his part of the mission. Once Group Two made way for them to enter, they would begin their search for Agni. Then the real questions would begin.

CHAPTER 14

Calida, Yuuna, and Beamer arrived at the border between Upper and Lower Ember. Yuuna, a Pyrocean girl with long waist-length blood-red hair, turned to Calida, "How do we know which building? There are many buildings here, and it's like the border is a city itself."

"Did the seer give any specifics?" Beamer asked, raising the thick black eyebrows that hovered over his honey eyes.

"Arrow didn't mention it, but we have to keep going. The other groups are going to be about thirty minutes behind us. That's all the time we have to locate the headquarters," Calida explained.

"Calida, thirty minutes is not a lot of time," Yuuna sighed.

"I didn't know it would look like this! I thought Lower Ember was completely run down. I was unaware that there were any developments."

"Is there any way to get a little more time? I mean we can't just run and jump into every little house on the border. That will really make a war," Beamer said.

"Let me cut that time down for you," a voice called. They looked down toward the first of several buildings to see Cahya.

"Cahya—" Calida started before seeing him put a finger to his lips and motion for them to join him. The trio quickly ran in his direction.

"Be quiet," Cahya said in a hushed voice as he motioned for them to follow him. They trailed Cahya, weaving through buildings as if they were bandits until they were closer to the center point of the border. He turned, took off his black hooded jacket, and gave it to Yuuna. "Cal, are you even thinking? Why would you bring Yuuna here? She'd be in danger just for the color of her hair. No one around here has red hair. And Pyroceans are hated here!"

"I forgot about that," Calida admitted.

Yuuna quickly put the hooded jacket on and covered her hair.

Cahya sighed, "I know where they are keeping Mom, but there's a problem. Aqila was on it when she said the border. Everyone who lives here is a supporter of Agni. Word on the street is that Agni got big money to build a community for his supporters. The houses aren't super fancy but they beat the run-down shacks everyone else lives in."

Cahya pointed as he continued. "Several times a day, they all go into that tall building toward the far side. The one that looks like a castle. Then many people from Lower Ember come and go as they please. It looks like Agni is providing food and money in exchange for support in Lower Ember. So we are seriously outnumbered. I set some traps last night to create a diversion that would bring everyone to the middle of the border. I saw Mom inside that building to the right. She's alone and in chains in a metal cell. I plan to heat the metal enough to be able to bend it and get her out."

"If it's just metal, how come she couldn't free herself? Is she waiting for something?" Yuuna asked.

Cahya and Calida slowly turned, giving her odd looks. The Pyrocean lowered her head, "Nevermind."

"Okay, the rest of the Flamethrowers are on their way here to help. Do you think Jai can get to Agni?" Calida asked.

Cahya shook his head. "I don't think anyone's getting to Agni without a fight. Calida, I don't think confronting Agni is a good move right now."

"We're here to help get your mom out. Calida and Arrow already made other plans to deal with Agni," Yuuna explained.

"Cal, I asked you to come with me last night. If you had, we would all be on the same page. I don't think messing with Agni right now is a good idea."

"Cahya, Jai feels ready to confront Agni to find out what he wants from him and why he wants him dead. We have to help him," Calida explained.

"But Agni is not just going to sit back and answer questions from Jai." Yuuna was puzzled.

"Why aren't you listening to Yuuna? This is not a good idea, but I'm not the leader, and it's impossible for you to listen to us, so fine," Cahya sighed. "All right then, let's get going." All of them, except for Beamer, made a quick dash for the building holding Sitara. Calida peeked in and gasped. She could see her mother's figure huddled in the corner, her face covered in bruises and her eyes filled with tears. The sight of her mother in such a state filled Calida with rage and helplessness. She wanted to scream and break the metal cage open, but she knew that wouldn't solve anything. The sight of her bruised hands made Calida's heart ache even more.

Cahya grabbed her. "It's going to be okay. I'm going to get her out of there. After I burn the bars, I'll melt the middle links of the chains. That should be enough to free her."

"They beat her . . . " Calida was distraught over seeing the cuts on her mother's face.

Cahya held her small hands inside his. "Nothing else horrible is going to happen on my watch. I swear on Dad's memory, nothing horrible will happen to this family. Trust me."

Calida nodded and went back to Yuuna.

"Wait, could we send her a signal to try burning it herself? Maybe—" Yuuna started but Calida raised her hand to quiet her. Beamer returned to the border to relay the information to the other groups when they arrived.

Groups Two and Three were fast approaching the border. "Stop, wait!" Beamer was running toward them.

Arrow ran to meet him. "What happened?"

"Nothing bad, just a big update. The border is infested with Agni's minions. Cahya located Sitara, and he already has a plan to free her. But about Agni, we're not going in and getting out without a major fight. We're completely outnumbered," Beamer explained.

Arrow turned to the rest of the Flamethrowers, "Everyone who wants to go forward, raise your hand." Every hand went up. Arrow turned to Beamer, "There you have it. We're going to Agni."

"All right then, follow me." Everyone carefully followed Beamer to the middle of the border town. "Okay, Cahya said that Agni is in that tall building over there." He pointed to the castle.

"There are so many people coming from Lower Ember, I guess, to meet with Agni," Jai noticed. "I had no clue that any development like this existed. All these little houses didn't use to be here. I was the town blacksmith and I never heard a word about anything like this."

"Maybe it's an inside secret. Only those with connections know about it," Beamer suggested.

"An entire city doesn't sound like a secret. Sounds like Jai didn't get around town much," Suvan spoke.

Jai nodded, "Well, you aren't wrong about that."

"All right, Group Two, go with Beamer to try and create an entrance for us. Beamer, you go back to Group One," Arrow instructed. Everyone nodded in agreement. Group Two followed Beamer toward the castle before he peeled off to return to his group.

The dark-gray stone castle towered over the semi-modern town, its imposing walls casting long shadows over the bustling streets below. The castle with towers on both sides seemed to be an ancient relic, a remnant of a time long past, yet it remained steadfast amid the changing world. The exterior was rough and rugged, pockmarked by centuries of wear and tear. Its walls were thick and imposing.

Arin and Alena went inside with the other visitors from Lower Ember as the doors opened for people to enter. A few minutes after the sisters went inside, Kiran and Flame followed.

"Okay, everybody's in." Arrow looked back at Jai and Suvan.

"How will we know when a path has been made?" Jai asked.

"Kiran recently developed a lightning proficiency and traded in his flame. He will send us the lightning signal," Arrow explained.

"Don't forget your hood, Jai. We don't want everybody to know you have little suns on your face." Suvan elbowed Jai in the rib. Jai nodded and put the black hood on, feeling the sting from Suvan's elbow. He rubbed his hands together, and upon feeling how sweaty and greasy they were, he realized his nerves were on fire. He didn't notice that Kiran came outside and made a small lightning pulse.

Arrow shot to his feet, surprising Jai, "That's the signal!" Arrow put on a dark-wine hooded cloak to cover his Pyrocean red hair and faint scales. The trio ran toward the door. Then slowing their pace, they walked in with the continuous stream of people coming inside from Lower Ember.

Suvan stayed by Jai's side the whole time. Arrow walked off with Kiran for a moment before rejoining them. "Kiran's going to make sure the next stage is clear for us," he whispered.

The castle's interior was just as impressive as its exterior. Dark, winding corridors led to countless rooms and chambers, each filled with artifacts and relics from the castle's long history. The main hall was large and opulent, with intricate tapestries and luxurious furnishings.

As the people packed the hall, everything went silent. A tall man appeared on the balcony. He wore a maroon hood, trimmed in black and a golden mask over his face with small openings for his eyes and mouth. His followers looked up to him with an air of reverence. His voice boomed, amplified by the acoustics of the chamber. The crowd cheered for him when he appeared, chanting his name. "Agni, Agni, Agni, Agni," was all that could be heard throughout the hall. Agni nodded and cleared his throat, calming and quieting the crowd.

The voice was distorted as he spoke through the golden mask. "Thank you for gathering here today. It thrills me to see your enthusiasm for our liberty mission. We will attack our enemy, the Pyroceans, at the close of the month. They have committed numerous atrocities on the Lower Ember border, killing our struggling soldiers as if we were animals! They walk around like gods, and we Emberites have had enough!

"My fellow disciples, we are on the cusp of a great revolution," Agni declared. "The time has come for us to rise and fight for our liberties and for justice, no matter the cost!" The crowd erupted into cheers, fists raised high in the air. Agni seemed to bask in the adulation as his words reverberated through the main hall.

"We are the chosen ones, destined to bring about a new world order," he continued. "We must not falter; we must not hesitate. The Legends, those false idols who have held sway over humanity for too long, must be eradicated from the face of the earth!" Agni's voice rose to a crescendo as he spoke, his words echoing off the walls. His followers chanted in unison, caught up in the fervor of his speech.

"We will not rest until our mission is complete. We will not stop until every last Legend has been purged from this world. We will fight, we will sacrifice, and we will prevail!"

The crowd yelled and cheered in agreement. Suvan nudged Jai. "Keep your gaze low."

Jai looked to Arrow, who had his hair carefully tied back and covered with the wine-colored hood. The Flamethrowers exchanged nervous glances as they all prayed that not a strand of his blood-red hair would be exposed. It was so packed in the main hall that an accidental bump could shift the hood and reveal a Pyrocean among the group.

Agni cleared his throat, and the crowd went quiet, "Yes, yes, my people. I know you are angry. With my leadership, we will be free! With my leadership, our pain will end. With my leadership, we will grow strong. Let us continue to gather our resources, so we can thrive and take the Pyroceans by surprise. We will catch their foolish young leader unaware and take a piece of their land while we're at it! The DragonLord only wants blood; he lives for bloodshed among the innocent."

Arrow looked angry, but he lowered his gaze to not give his amber eyes away. Agni continued, "After we put the Pyroceans in their place, we will add Kindle to our fold, and we will be one! Finally, we will have true unity! We will break the chains of injustice that those idols calling themselves Legends have wrapped around our necks. We will free ourselves from the curse of Cyra!"

Agni's voice softened. "I hope everyone is settling into our little community nicely. I know the homes are small, but know that bigger things will come. We are only just beginning to taste the reward of our labor, and these little houses are an upgrade in themselves from huts and homelessness. So, my people, await my instructions; everything will be ready within a couple of weeks. Gather yourselves, steel your nerves, and prepare for war! Peasants, they call us. Peasants will fight dragons, and we will win!" Agni walked away from the balcony as the crowd chanted his name.

"Now's our chance. Everyone is starting to disperse," Arrow whispered.

Suvan looked up, "Kiran just made another signal."

Arrow nodded, "I know—I saw."

The trio separated briefly, each stealthily taking his turn up the stairs. Once they were all upstairs, Kiran left, moving to the next area. "Suvan, stay with Jai," Arrow instructed before he left, going toward the right. Suvan and Jai carefully proceeded to the left. They hid by the edge of the balcony.

Bang! Bang! Bang! The sound of distant explosives echoed through the castle. A loud commotion followed. Agni appeared from a hallway. A guard ran toward him. "Agni, bombs went off at central headquarters!"

"Take half of your men to address it. Keep all fires contained. Something seems off. I can feel it. Bring any remnants of the bombs to the boy. He should be able to tell where it came from and how it was made. He may even be able to create an upgrade for our cause," Agni explained.

"Um, sir, which boy?"

"Arka's assistant—that boy is quite resourceful," Agni continued.

"Zay," Jai whispered, shaking his head. Suvan elbowed him in the ribs, reminding him to keep still.

Another of Agni's minions ran up to him. "Agni, Dehateh's wife—she's escaped!"

"I'm not surprised. She probably burned herself out. I told you to keep her guarded," Agni seemed strangely calm.

"We did, but we sent those guards to central headquarters," the man explained.

Agni laughed. "This is interesting. I knew something was up. I would not have suspected something so elaborate. Let the woman run; I have most of what I need. Arka's boy gave it to me. Go and handle the disturbance at the central headquarters."

"Yes sir!" they both said in unison as they left.

Agni laughed while walking away.

Jai turned to Suvan. "Now's our chance."

Suvan shook his head. "We have to wait for Arrow's lead."

"What if he gets away? He already knows that something is up," Jai questioned.

"We still have to follow the chain of command," Suvan explained. Jai's soul was itching to act.

The pair darted into a vacant room. Kiran saw them from his angle in the hall and signaled them to come out. They ran to the back of the second floor. However, Agni was nowhere to be seen.

"Well, who would have thought we'd cross paths so soon, Firefly."

Zay stood tall, his muscles taut and ready for action. He wore a look of fierce determination on his face, his eyes locked onto Jai's. His fists were tightly clenched; he cracked his knuckles with anticipation.

Jai and Suvan turned around, "What do you want, Zay?"

Zay leaned calmly on the stone wall behind him and shrugged his shoulders, "I'm here getting my orders from Agni," he started unrolling a small piece of paper. "I mean, we could always finish what we started in the forge. Or did you forget how it felt to be strangled with a bowstring?"

"What does he want with me?" Jai asked.

Zay's eyes went wide before returning to normal, "At this point, he probably wants your head severed from your body."

Suvan jumped in front of Jai. "Well, he's not getting it." He punched a round of fire toward Zay, but it was futile. Zay used his superb agility to avoid every attack before throwing a smoke bomb at them. Jai and Suvan coughed and gasped for air; their nostrils filled with so much smoke, they nearly collapsed.

Chaos followed, and screaming and shouting ensued.

"Jai, Suvan, follow the sound of my voice—" Flame started. The pair ran right, following Flame's teenage voice. The smoke screen cleared as they continued right. However, Flame, the teenage boy with curly black hair and light brown eyes, lay on the ground motionless. He could not have been more than fourteen years old.

"Flame!" Suvan called, running to him. As Suvan lifted his shoulders off the ground, his hands became covered in crimson red. The boy's eyes were glassy and unfocused. His face went from contorted in pain to completely still.

Arrow ran toward them and stopped when he saw the teenager's lifeless body. He shook with anger. "We kill as many of them as possible," Arrow growled. The jade scales near his eyes glowed, fangs grew from his mouth, and he released a feral roar. The gurgling sound echoed through the castle. He pulled an arrow from his quiver and shot at the roof, causing it to ignite.

"Wait! I might be able to save him!" Jai went to Suvan, who held Flame's bloody body. He opened his hands and revealed a glittering golden light. He placed his hands on Flame's wounds. Jai was trying to heal what he could. He couldn't take his time as he did with Arrow. The light consumed the wound on Flame. It slowly began to heal the wound. The blood was beginning to dissipate, and the flesh was trying to close over the gaping wound.

I need more time!

Agni's minions began to flank them on either side. Arrow shot flaming arrows and took down Agni's soldiers as quickly as possible. "Jai, I'm trying to buy you some time!" he shouted. Then Arrow roared, and a raging fire escaped from his mouth, quickly burning everything as far as he could see.

Suddenly, they heard Alena screaming.

"Arrow, I'm going to them," Suvan called as he ran off toward the scream. The soldiers began to push back on

Arrow a bit. Jai lifted his head and sent a blinding ray of light to knock off a few soldiers on Arrow's heels. Flame's wound was critical, and Jai needed to move him. He lifted Flame over his shoulder with ease and began to run in a seemingly clear direction.

He darted into the next room, laid Flame down carefully, and continued to heal him. The wound was almost closed. Flame's childlike eyes began to flutter. A wave of peace and purpose washed over Jai.

Slowly Flame sat up, "I made it," he whispered before crumpling into Jai's arms unconscious once more.

Jai smiled. Suddenly, he felt a presence. Learning from the last time he was heedless, Jai stood tall and turned around to face the golden mask. Hate and dread consumed him at once.

"Agni," Jai spat.

He chuckled, confidently taking a step closer, "It seems you've been eager to meet me, Legend."

As Jai stared at that golden mask, it was as if his consciousness traveled through time. A dreadful feeling began to rise, but he crushed it. His body was radiating like a rising fire. He could feel his power growing with every step he took, his muscles rippling under his skin as he prepared to face off against Agni. He felt a roaring fire grow within him. A fire that wanted to consume; a fire that wanted to be free.

As they stood facing each other, Jai couldn't help but think of her. It was like he was channeling a revelation from a previous life. In the back of his mind, Jai reflected on the shimmering silver eyes. And he instantly knew that everything she said had been right. He didn't need a new vision. The one she gave him was sufficient. There was nothing to know besides this moment. There was nothing new to be understood. That little fire within him that was constantly seeking its purpose finally found its fuel.

Jai had always felt a little fire burning deep within him. It was a constant ember that flickered—never quite extinguished, but never quite fully ignited either. For years, he had questioned his purpose. But as he stood there with Flame, barely conscious beside his feet, he felt something within him shift. That little fire inside him was suddenly no longer a mere ember but a roaring inferno that burned with a fierce intensity. It pulsed through his veins, filling him with an energy that he had never known before.

Jai stood tall, his eyes fixed on his opponent, his body poised for action. He could feel the heat of his inner fire rushing to every limb of his body, screaming to become a tangible force to end Agni. Jai's eyes began to glow.

Ignite!

Fire covered Agni's hands. Jai wielded fire in one hand and light in the other. They each summoned their elements at the same time. Fire and light clashed in a vibrant wall. Wild embers erupted, setting small fires around the room. Jai could feel Agni's power as some of the embers of his powerful flames pushed through the beaming light and burned Jai's shoulder. But he couldn't feel pain, only anger. The forces repelled each other, knocking the two into opposite walls.

"What do you want from me?"

"To help you right a wrong. To free our people from a cycle of hell you are bound to continue. To save the world, by sacrificing those who are destined to destroy it. You. Must. Die."

ON THE WAY TO THEYRA

The young woman was comfortably perched upon the back of her massive owl. Her piercing silver eyes enjoyed the view of the world beneath her. Delicate strands of gray hair twirled behind her in the hot, dry wind. Talon's wings beat with powerful strokes, propelling them forward through the sky. Aqila loved the sound of the wild wind rushing past her face.

She opened her arms to the sky as her legs held their grip on Talon's feathery back. She could feel the strong muscles of her dasher moving beneath her. The sun beat down upon her, its warmth seeping into her bones, and she felt an exhilarating sense of freedom as she soared through the air. His flapping wings were a lovely melody on a beautiful day. Talon soared higher and higher, climbing toward the clouds. Aqila embraced that familiar rush of adrenaline, feeling a deep connection with the owl beneath her. She could sense his power and grace, his freedom and wildness.

As the great bird edged her closer to the Landkeepers' territory, she couldn't shake the odd feeling she had about Jai. She was positive they had never met before, but the way his golden eyes gently glowed in the light seemed so familiar to her. They had only just met, but Aqila felt deeply connected to him. She wished they could have spent just a bit more time together, but the reality of their separate lives had intervened.

A searing headache shook her from her blissful thoughts. Talon stiffened and instinctively slowed his pace. Feeling as if her brain was being twisted from her head, Aqila rubbed her temples. Her owl squawked loudly.

"It's okay, Talon! I'm okay; let's hurry to Theyra. A vision is coming."

Together they flew across the light-blue canvas peppered with white clouds. As they continued their journey, the headache never ebbed, and a subtle dreadful sensation caused a shiver to run along her spine.

Whatever this vision is, it cannot be good.

Far away in the eastern mountains of Kashmala, a middle-aged woman made her way to a house. The clouds were so close she felt as if she could touch them. She was not thrilled to be this high in the sky; however, the sun's ray gently danced upon her aging skin. She squinted her golden eyes and smiled. Those warm rays energized her entire being.

Reluctantly, her footsteps brought her to the pale-blue front door. Her vision blurred as her heartbeat quickened. Her hand trembled as she slowly lifted it to the door.

With an exasperated sigh, she dropped her head and her hand fell to her side.

Suddenly, the door opened.

She tilted her head up to meet the dark-gray gaze of the seven-foot-tall man. He smiled, running his brown hands through his curly bright-gray hair.

"Come in, Cyra. I was expecting you."

She chuckled, "Of course you were, Zeroun."

Slowly she stepped inside. Trembling uncontrollably, she lost her balance. Her vision became more blurry to the point she could barely see anything. Zeroun carefully led her by the hand to sit down.

"How was the journey here?"

"I really don't have time for small talk," she sighed.

Sighing heavily, "I understand. I—I know why you're here. Tell me what you need to see."

"My heart feels heavy. I know I've done some terrible things. I just ... I tried to redeem myself. I've done the repentance prayer just as Basir suggested. I don't know if it was accepted by the Heavens. Will I ascend to the Stars? Maybe I could guide her."

"I can't give you an exact answer to that. But I can use the sight to get a glimpse of the lasting repercussions."

"Please do," she pleaded.

"Before I start -"

"Please Zeroun, I must do something! I don't have much time! I must know what to do!"

"All right," he whispered.

Cyra listened to his soft chanting. His soothing voice brought ease to her soul. She slowly exhaled as a wave of serenity washed over her.

Zeroun whispered, "Heavenly Skies, show me what I seek. Glorious Heavens, expand my sight as you see fit."

Zeroun inhaled sharply, and his gray eyes began to glow. Besides the soft sounds of their breathing, all was quiet. Slowly, Cyra brought her hand to her heart and gently patted herself. Her palms were sweating and her body would tremble at random moments.

Several moments passed, but Zeroun was quiet.

Maybe there's nothing that can be done for me.

Cyra rubbed her knees before standing up slowly. She blinked several times, attempting to clear the emerging tears.

The Stars have abandoned me. I've gone too far.

"Cyra," Zeroun called softly to her.

"If there was nothing to see, I understand, Zeroun. I just appreciate all you have done for us."

"Cyra, I did see something. If you will take a seat, I'll explain it."

"If it's bad news, I'd rather just accept death."

"I thought you were seeking closure. Not just for you, but for her too. If that's what you want, that's what I have."

Zeroun guided Cyra to sit once more. "Based on what I saw, you will enter the void."

"What?"

"It's not often talked about. Most people are only conscious of ascension and total death. You haven't done enough to reach ascension because your actions have triggered a blood curse."

"A blood curse? That would affect my descendants... Soleil," she sighed.

"Yes, the die was set long ago. At this point, there is nothing that can be done about the curse itself. It's a curse of twos. It will activate in the second-born child of your future descendants."

"And Soleil?"

"The curse will start with her..."

"How is that possible? Soleil doesn't have a gift. I thought that was the punishment that Aenon and I had to endure."

"In the near future, a chaotic power will awaken in Soleil. She will suffer, and her descendants will be powerful. The second born will be gifted with exceptional abilities that they will struggle to control. Solar eclipses will awaken the curse in full force. It will be likened to a summoning of chaos. Down the line, some will be strong enough to resist the full effects of the curse, but most will not. Death by lightning will be unavoidable until the curse is broken. I'm sorry, Cyra, this one won't be simple to break."

"When will it be broken?"

"Unfortunately, I did not see that in our lifetime."

Tears streamed down Cyra's face. "What have I done? How can I stop it? There must be something I can do! It's not fair that several generations of my descendants will suffer for what I and Aenon have done. Please, Zeroun, what can I do?"

He touched her shoulder, "I—I couldn't see that far. The solution surpasses our lifetime. I'm sorry, Cyra; I only see hard decisions with equally difficult consequences for you. The only thing you can do is to try and help Soleil... or end her. At this point, you will not ascend regardless of the path you choose. However, the void is a better fate than total death. I know this revelation is heavy, but I urge you to endure."

Cyra stood hastily, violently wiping her tears, "Thank you, Zeroun. I will take my leave."

"Of course, Cyra."